Cyril perceived as in a flash of understanding that it was they *who were being married!*

There had been some terrible, unexplainable mistake, and he was stupidly standing in another man's place, taking life vows upon himself! The thing had passed from an advantage of little moment into a matter of life-tragedy, two life-tragedies perhaps! What should he do?

Then, with his question, came the words, "I now pronounce you husband and wife," and "let no man put asunder what God has joined."

THE BEST MAN

LIVING BOOKS®
Tyndale House Publishers, Inc.
Wheaton, Illinois

This Tyndale House book
by Grace Livingston Hill
contains the complete text
of the original hardcover edition.
NOT ONE WORD
HAS BEEN OMITTED.

Printing History
J. B. Lippincott edition published 1908
Tyndale House edition/1989

Library of Congress Catalog Card Number 89-50250
ISBN 0-8423-0371-5

1 2 3 4 5 6 7 8 94 93 92 91 90 89

CYRIL Gordon had been seated at his desk but ten minutes and was deep in the morning's mail when there came an urgent message from his chief, summoning him to an immediate audience in the inner office.

The chief had keen blue eyes and shaggy eyebrows. He never wasted words; yet those words when spoken had more weight than those of most other men in Washington.

There was the briefest of good-morning gleams in his nod and glance, but he only said:

"Gordon, can you take the Pennsylvania train for New York that leaves the station in thirty-two minutes?"

The young man was used to abrupt questions from his chief, but he caught his breath, mentally surveying his day as it had been planned:

"Why, sir, I suppose I could—if it is necessary—" He hesitated.

"It is necessary," said the chief curtly, as if that settled the matter.

"But—half an hour!" ejaculated Gordon in dismay. "I could hardly get to my rooms and back to the station. I don't see how—Isn't there a train a little later?"

"Later train won't do. Call up your man on the 'phone. Tell him to pack your bag and meet you at the station in twenty minutes. You'll need evening clothes. Can you depend on your man to get your things quickly without fail?"

There was that in the tone of the chief that caused Gordon to make no further demur.

"Sure!" he responded with his usual businesslike tone, as he strode to the 'phone. His daze was passing off. "Evening clothes?" he questioned curiously, as if he might not have heard aright.

"Yes, evening clothes," was the curt answer, "and everything you'll need for daytime for a respectable gentleman of leisure — a tourist, you understand."

Gordon perceived that he was being given a mission of trust and importance, not unmixed with mystery perhaps. He was new in the Secret Service, and it had been his ambition to rise in his chief's good graces. He rang the telephone bell furiously and called up the number of his own apartments, giving his man orders in a breezy, decisive tone that caused a look of satisfaction to settle about the fine wrinkles of the chief's eyes.

Gordon's watch was out and he was telling his man on just what car he must leave the apartments for the station. The chief noted it was two cars ahead of what would have been necessary. His gray head gave an almost imperceptible nod of commendation, and his eyes showed that he was content with his selection of a man.

"Now, sir," said Gordon, as he hung up the receiver, "I'm ready for orders."

"Well, you are to go to New York, and take a cab for the Cosmopolis Hotel — your room there is already secured by wire. Your name is John Burnham. The name of the hotel and the number of your room are on this memorandum. You will find awaiting you an invitation to dine this evening with a Holman, who knows of you as an expert in code-reading. Our men met him on the train an hour ago and arranged that he should invite you. He didn't know whom they represented, of course. He has already tried to 'phone you at the hotel about coming to dinner to-night. He knows you are expected there before evening. Here is a letter of introduction to him from a man he knows. Our men got that also. It is genuine, of course.

"Last night a message of national importance, written in cipher, was stolen from one of our men before it had been read. This is now in the hands of Holman, who is hoping to have you decipher it for him and a few guests who will also be present at dinner. They wish to use it for their own purposes. Your commission is to get hold of the message and bring it to us as soon as possible. Another message of very different import, written upon the same kind of paper, is in this envelope, with a translation for you to use in case you have to substitute a message. You will have to use your own wits and judgment. The main thing is, *get the paper, and get back with it,* with as little delay as possible. Undoubtedly your life will be in danger should it be discovered that you have made off with it. Spare no care to protect yourself *and the message,* at all hazards. Remember, I said, *and the message,* young man! It means much to the country.

"In this envelope is money—all you will probably need. Telegraph or 'phone to this address if you are in trouble. Draw on us for more, if necessary, also through this same address. Here is the code you can use in case you find it necessary to telegraph. Your ticket is already bought. I have sent Clarkson to the station for it, and he will meet you at the train. You can give him instructions in case you find you have forgotten anything. Take your mail with you, and telegraph back orders to your stenographer. I think that is all. Oh, yes, to-night, while you are at dinner, you will be called to the 'phone by one of our men. If you are in trouble, this may give you opportunity to get away, and put us wise. You will find a motor at the door now, waiting to take you to the station. If your man doesn't get there with your things, take the train any way, and buy some more when you get to New York. Don't turn aside from your commission for anything. Don't let *anything* hinder you! Make it a matter of life and death! Good morning, and good luck!"

The chief held out a big, hairy hand that was surprisingly warm and soft considering the hardness of his face and voice, and the young man grasped it, feeling as if he were suddenly being plunged into waves of an unknown depth and he would fain hold on to this strong hand.

He went out of the office quietly enough, and the keen old eyes watched him knowingly, understanding the beating of the heart under Gordon's well-fitting business coat, the mingled elation and dread over the commission. But there had been no hesitancy, no question of acceptance, when the nature of the the the commission was made known. The young man was "game." He would do. Not even an eyelash had flickered at the hint of danger. The chief felt he would be faithful even in the face of possible death.

Gordon's man came rushing into the station just after he reached there himself. Clarkson was already there with the ticket. Gordon had time to scribble a message to Julia Bentley, whose perfumed scrawl he had read on the way down. Julia had bidden him to her presence that evening. He could not tell whether he was relieved or sorry to tell her he could not come. It began to look to him a good deal as if he would ask Julia Bentley to marry him some day, when she got tired of playing all the others off against him, and he could make up his mind to surrender his freedom to any woman.

He bought a paper and settled himself comfortably in the parlor car, but his interest was not in the paper. His strange commission engaged all his thoughts. He took out the envelope containing instructions and went over the matter, looking curiously at the cipher message and its translation, which, however, told him nothing. It was the old chief's way to keep the business to himself until such time as he chose to explain. Doubtless it was safer for both message and messenger that he did not know the full import of what he was undertaking.

Gordon carefully noted down everything that his chief had told him, comparing it with the written instructions in the envelope; arranged in his mind just how he could proceed when he reached New York; tried to think out a good plan for recovering the stolen message, but could not; and so decided to trust to the inspiration of the moment. Then it occurred to him to clear his overcoat pockets of any letters or other tell-tale articles and stow them in his suit-case. He might have to leave his overcoat behind him. So it would be well to have no clues for anyone to follow.

Having arranged these matters, and prepared a few letters with notes for his stenographer, to be mailed back to her from Philadelphia, he reread Julia Bentley's note. When every angular line of her tall script was imprinted on his memory, he tore the perfumed note into tiny pieces and dropped them from the car window.

The question was, did he or did he not want to ask Julia Bentley to become his wife? He had no doubt as to what her answer would be. Julia had made it pretty plain to him that she would rather have him than any of her other admirers; though she did like to keep them all attendant upon her. Well, that was her right so long as she was unmarried. He had no fault to find with her. She was a fine girl, and everybody liked her. Also, she was of a good family, and with a modest fortune in her own right. Everybody was taking it for granted that they liked each other. It was time he was married and had a real home, he supposed, whatever that was—that seemed to have so great a charm for all his friends. To his eyes, it had as yet taken on no alluring mirage effect. He had never known a real home, more than his quiet bachelor apartments were to him now, where his man ordered everything as he was told, and the meals were sent up when wanted. He had money enough from his inheritance to make things more than comfortable, and he was deeply interested in the profession he had chosen.

Still, if he was ever going to marry, it was high time, of course. But did he want Julia? He could not quite make it seem pleasant to think of her in his rooms when he came home at night tired; she would always be wanting to go to her endless theatre parties and receptions and dances; always be demanding his attention. She was bright and handsome and well dressed, but he had never made love to her. He could not quite imagine himself doing so. How did men make love, any way? Could one call it love when it was "made" love? These questions followed one another idly through his brain as the landscape whirled past him. If he had stayed at home, he would have spent the evening with Julia, as she requested in her note, and there would probably have been a quiet half-hour after other callers had gone when he would have stayed as he had been doing of late, and tried to find out whether he really cared for her or not.

Suppose, for instance, they were married, and she sat beside him now. Would any glad thrill fill his heart as he looked at her beautiful face and realized that she was his? He tried to look over toward the next chair and imagine that the tired, fat old lady with the double chin and the youthful purple hat was Julia, but that would not work. He whirled his chair about and tried it on an empty chair. That went better; but still no thrill of joy lifted him out of his sordid self. He could not help thinking about little trying details. The way Julia looked when she was vexed. Did one mind that in the woman one loved? The way she ordered her coachman about. Would she ever speak so to her husband? She had a charming smile, but her frown was — well — unbecoming to say the least.

He tried to keep up the fallacy of her presence. He bought a magazine that he knew she liked, and read a story to her (in imagination). He could easily tell how her black eyes would snap at certain phrases she disliked. He knew just what her comment would be upon the heroine's conduct.

It was an old disputed point between them. He knew how she would criticize the hero, and somehow he felt himself in the hero's place every time she did it. The story had not been a success, and he felt a weariness as he laid the magazine aside at the call for dinner from the dining-car.

Before he had finished his luncheon he had begun to feel that though Julia might think now that she would like to marry him, the truth about it was that she would not enjoy the actual life together any better than he would. Were all marriages like that? Did people lose the glamour and just settle down to endure each other's faults and make the most of each other's pleasant side, and not have anything more? Or was he getting cynical? Had he lived alone too long, as his friends sometimes told him, and so was losing the ability really to love anybody but himself? He knit his brows, and got up whistling to go out and see why the train had stopped so long in this little country settlement.

It was just beyond Princeton, and they were not far now from New York. It would be most annoying to be delayed so near to his destination. He was anxious to get things in train for his evening of hard work. It was necessary to find out how the land lay as soon as possible.

It appeared that there was a wrecked freight ahead of them, and there would be delay. No one knew just how long; it would depend on how soon the wrecking train arrived to help.

Gordon walked nervously up and down the grass at the side of the track, looking anxiously each way for sign of the wrecking train. The thought of Julia did occur to him, but he put it impatiently away, for he knew just how poorly Julia would bear a delay on a journey even in his company. He had been with her once when the engine got off the track on a short trip down to a Virginia houseparty, and she was the most impatient creature alive, although it mattered not one whit to any of the rest of the party whether they made merry on the train or at their friend's house. And yet, if Julia were anything at all to him, would not he like the thought of her companionship now?

A great white dog hobbled up to him and fawned upon him as he turned to go back to the train, and he laid his hand kindly upon the animal's head, and noted the wistful eyes upon his face. He was a noble dog, and Gordon stood for a moment fondling him. Then he turned impatiently and tramped back to his car again. But when he reached the steps he found that the dog had followed him.

Gordon frowned, half in annoyance, half in amusement, and sitting down on a log by the wayside he took the dog's pink nozzle into his hands, caressing the white fur above it gently.

The dog whined happily, and Gordon meditated. How long would the train wait? Would he miss getting to New York in time for the dinner? Would he miss the chance to rise in the chief's good graces? The chief would expect him to get to New York some other way if the train were delayed. How long ought he to wait on possibilities?

All at once he saw the conductor and trainmen coming back hurriedly. Evidently the train was about to start. With a final kindly stroke of the white head, he called a workman nearby, handed him half a dollar to hold the dog, and sprang on board.

He had scarcely settled himself into his chair, however, before the dog came rushing up the aisle from the other end of the car, and precipitated himself muddily and noisily upon him.

With haste and perturbation Gordon hurried the dog to the door and tried to fling him off, but the poor creature pulled back and clung to the platform yelping piteously.

Just then the conductor came from the other car and looked at him curiously.

"No dogs allowed in these cars," he said gruffly.

"Well, if you know how to enforce that rule I wish you

would," said Gordon. "I'm sure I don't know what to do with him."

"Where has he been since you left Washington?" asked the grim conductor with suspicion in his eyes.

"I certainly haven't had him secreted about me, a dog of that size," remarked the young man dryly. "Besides, he isn't my dog. I never saw him before till he followed me at the station. I'm as anxious to be rid of him as he is to stay."

The conductor eyed the young man keenly, and then allowed a grim sense of humor to appear in one corner of his mouth.

"Got a chain or a rope for him?" he asked more sympathetically.

"Well, no," remarked the unhappy attaché of the dog. "Not having had an appointment with the dog I didn't provide myself with a leash for him."

"Take him into the baggage car," said the conductor briefly, and slammed his way into the next car.

There seemed nothing else to be done, but it was most annoying to be thus forced on the notice of his fellow-travellers, when his commission required that he be as inconspicuous as possible.

At Jersey City he hoped to escape and leave the dog to the tender mercies of the baggage man, but that official was craftily waiting for him and handed the animal over to his unwilling master with a satisfaction ill-proportioned to the fee he had received for caring for him.

Then began a series of misfortunes. Disappointment and suspicion stalked beside him, and behind him a voice continually whispered his chief's last injunction: "Don't let anything hinder you!"

Frantically he tried first one place and then another, but all to no effect. Nobody apparently wanted to care for a stray white dog, and his very haste aroused suspicion. Once he came near being arrested as a dog thief. He could not get rid of that dog! Yet he must not let him follow him! Would he have to have the animal sent home to Washington as the only solution of the problem? Then a queer fancy seized him that just in some such way had Miss Julia Bentley been shadowing his days for nearly three years now; and he had actually this very day been considering calmly whether he might not have to marry her just because she was so persistent in her taking possession of him. Not that she was unladylike, of course; no, indeed! She was stately and beautiful, and had never offended. But she had always quietly, persistently, taken it for granted that he would be her attendant whenever she chose; and she always chose whenever he was in the least inclined to enjoy any other woman's company.

He frowned at himself. Was there something weak about his character that a woman or a dog could so easily master him? Would any other employee in the office, once trusted with his great commission, have allowed it to be hindered by a dog?

Gordon could not afford to waste any more time. He must get rid of him at once!

The express office would not take a dog without a collar and chain unless he was crated; and the delays and exasperating hindrances seemed to be interminable. But at last, following the advice of a kindly officer, he took the dog to an institution in New York where, he was told, dogs were boarded and cared for, and where he finally disposed of him, having first paid ten dollars for the privilege. As he settled back in a taxicab with his watch in his hand, he congratulated himself that he had still ample time to reach his hotel and get into evening dress before he must present himself for his work.

Within three blocks of the hotel the cab came to such a sudden standstill that Gordon was thrown to his knees.

2

THEY were surrounded immediately by a crowd in which policemen were a prominent feature. The chauffeur seemed dazed in the hands of the officers.

A little, barefoot, white-faced figure huddled limply in the midst showed Gordon what had happened: also there were menacing glances toward himself and a show of lifted stones. He heard one boy say: "You bet he's in a hurry to git away. Them kind allus is. They don't care who they kills, they don't!"

A great horror seized him. The cab had run over a newsboy and perhaps killed him. Yet instantly came the remembrance of his commission: "Don't let anything hinder you. Make it a matter of life and death!" Well, it looked as if this was a matter of death that hindered him now.

They bundled the moaning boy into the taxicab and as Gordon saw no escape through the tightly packed crowd, who eyed him suspiciously, he climbed in beside the grimy little scrap of unconscious humanity, and they were off to the hospital to the tune of "Don't let anything hinder you! Don't let anything hinder you!" until Gordon felt that if it did not stop soon he would go crazy. He meditated opening the cab door and making his escape in spite of the speed they were making, but a vision of broken legs and a bed in the hospital for himself held him to his seat. One of the policemen had climbed on in front with the chauffeur, and now and again he glanced back as if he were conveying a couple of prisoners to jail. It was vexatious beyond anything! And all on account of that white dog! Could anything be more ridiculous than the whole performance?

His annoyance and irritation almost made him forget that it was his progress through the streets that had silenced this mite beside him. But just as he looked at his watch for the fifth time the boy opened his eyes and moaned, and there was in those eyes a striking resemblance to the look in the eyes of the dog of whose presence he had but just rid himself.

Gordon started. In spite of himself it seemed as if the dog were reproaching him through the eyes of the child. Then suddenly the boy spoke.

"Will yous stay by me till I'm mended?" whispered the weak little voice.

Gordon's heart leaped in horror again, and it came to him that he was being tried out this day to see if he had the right stuff in him for hard tasks. The appeal in the little street-boy's eyes reached him as no request had ever yet done, and yet he might not answer it. Duty,—life and death duty,— called him elsewhere, and he must leave the little fellow whom he had been the involuntary cause of injuring, to suffer and per-haps to die. It cut him to the quick not to respond to that ur-gent appeal.

Was it because he was weary that he was visited just then by a vision of Julia Bentley with her handsome lips curled scornfully? Julia Bentley would not have approved of his stopping to carry a boy to the hospital, any more than to care for a dog's comfort.

"Look here, kiddie," he said gently, leaning over the child, "I'd stay by you if I could, but I've already made myself later for an appointment by coming so far with you. Do you know what Duty is?"

The child nodded sorrowfully.

"Don't yous mind me," he murmured weakly. "Just yous go. I'm game all right." Then the voice trailed off into silence again, and the eyelids fluttered down upon the little, grimy, unconscious face.

Gordon went into the hospital for a brief moment to leave some money in the hands of the authorities for the benefit of the boy, and a message that he would return in a week or two if possible; then hurried away.

Back in the cab once more, he felt as if he had killed a man and left him lying by the roadside while he continued his unswerving march toward the hideous duty which was growing increasingly more portentous, and to be relieved of which he would gladly have surrendered further hope of his chief's favor. He closed his eyes and tried to think, but all the time the little white face of the child came before his vision, and the mocking eyes of Julia Bentley tantalized him, as if she were telling him that he had spoiled all his chances — and hers — by his foolish soft-heartedness. Though, what else could he have done than he had done, he asked himself fiercely.

He looked at his watch. It was at least ten minutes' ride to the hotel, the best time they could make. Thanks to his man the process of dressing for the evening would not take long, for he knew that everything would be in place and he would not be hindered. He would make short work of his toilet. But there was his suit-case. It would not do to leave it at the hotel, neither must he take it with him to the house where he was to be a guest. There was nothing for it but to go around by the way of the station where it would have to be checked. That meant a longer ride and more delay, but it must be done.

Arrived at the hotel at last, and in the act of signing the unaccustomed "John Burnham" in the hotel registry, there came a call to the telephone.

With a hand that trembled from excitement he took the

receiver. His breath went from him as though he had just run up five flights of stairs. "Yes? Hello! Oh, Mrs. Holman. Yes! Burnham. I've but just arrived. I was delayed. A wreck ahead of the train. Very kind of you to invite me, I'm sure. Yes, I'll be there in a few moments, as soon as I can get rid of the dust of travel. Thank you. Good-bye."

It all sounded very commonplace to the clerk, who was making out bills and fretting because he could not get off to take his girl to the theatre that night, but as Gordon hung up the receiver he looked around furtively as if expecting to see a dozen detectives ready to seize upon him. It was the first time he had ever undertaken a commission under an assumed name and he felt as if he were shouting his commission through the streets of New York.

The young man made short work of his toilet. Just as he was leaving the hotel a telegram was handed him. It was from his chief, and so worded that to the operator who had copied it down it read like a hasty call to Boston; but to his code-enlightened eyes it was merely a blind to cover his exit from the hotel and from New York, and set any possible hunters on a wrong scent. He marvelled at the wonderful mind of his chief, who thought out every detail of an important campaign, and forgot not one little possible point where difficulty might arise.

Gordon had a nervous feeling as he again stepped into a taxicab and gave his order. He wondered how many stray dogs, and newsboys with broken legs, would attach themselves to him on the way to dinner. Whenever the speed slowed down, or they were halted by cars and autos, his heart pounded painfully, lest something new had happened, but he arrived safely and swiftly at the station, checked his suitcase, and took another cab to the residence of Mr. Holman, without further incident.

The company were waiting for him, and after the introductions they went immediately to the dining-room. Gordon took his seat with the feeling that he had bungled everything hopelessly, and had arrived so late that there was no possible hope of his doing what he had been sent to do. For the first few minutes his thoughts were a jumble, and his eyes dazed with the brilliant lights of the room. He could not single out the faces of the people present and differentiate them one from another. His heart beat painfully against the stiff expanse of evening linen. It almost seemed as if those near him could hear it. He found himself starting and stammering when he was addressed as "Mr. Burnham." His thoughts were mingled with white dogs, newsboys, and ladies with scornful smiles.

He was seated on the right of his hostess, and gradually her gentle manners gave him quietness. He began to gain control of himself, and now he seemed to see afar the keen eye of his chief watching the testing of his new commissioner. His heart swelled to meet the demand made upon him. A strong purpose came to him to rise above all obstacles and conquer in spite of circumstances. He must forget everything else and rise to the occasion.

From that moment the dancing lights that multiplied themselves in the glittering silver and cut glass of the table began to settle into order; and slowly, one by one, the conglomeration of faces around the board resolved itself into individuals.

There was the pretty, pale hostess, whose gentle ways seemed hardly to fit with her large, boisterous, though polished husband. Unscrupulousness was written all over his ruddy features, also a certain unhidden craftiness which passed for geniality among his kind.

There were two others with faces full of cunning, both men of wealth and culture. One did not think of the word "refinement" in connection with them; still, that might be conceded also, but it was all dominated by the cunning that on this occasion, at least, was allowed to sit unmasked upon their countenances. They had outwitted an enemy, and they were openly exultant.

Of the other guests, one was very young and sleek, with eyes that had early learned to evade; one was old and weary-looking, with a hunted expression; one was thick-set, with little eyes set close in a fat, selfish face. Gordon began to understand that these three but did the bidding of the others. They listened to the conversation merely from a business standpoint and not with any personal interest. They were there because they were needed, and not because they were desired.

There was one bond which they seemed to hold in common: an alert readiness to combine for their mutual safety. This did not manifest itself in anything tangible, but the guest felt that it was there and ready to spring upon him at any instant.

All this came gradually to the young man as the meal with its pleasant formalities began. As yet nothing had been said about the reason for his being there.

"Did you tell me you were in a wreck?" suddenly asked the hostess sweetly, turning to him, and the table talk hushed instantly while the host asked: "A wreck! Was it serious?"

Gordon perceived his mistake at once. With instant caution, he replied smilingly, "Oh, nothing serious, a little break-down on a freight ahead, which required time to patch up. It reminded me — " and then he launched boldly into one of the bright dinner stories for which he was noted among his companions at home. His heart was beating wildly, but he succeeded in turning the attention of the table to his joke, instead of to asking from where he had come and on what road. Questions about himself were dangerous he plainly saw, if he would get possession of the valued paper and get away without leaving a trail behind him. He succeeded in one thing more, which, though he did not know it, was the very thing his chief had hoped he would do when he chose him instead of a man who had wider experience: he made every man at the table feel that he was delightful, a man to be thoroughly trusted and enjoyed; who would never suspect them of having any ulterior motives in anything they were doing.

The conversation for a little time rippled with bright stories and repartee, and Gordon began to feel almost as if he were merely enjoying a social dinner at home, with Julia Bentley down the table listening and haughtily smiling her approval. For the time the incidents of the dog and the newsboy were forgotten, and the young man felt his self-respect rising. His heart was beginning to get into normal action again and he could control his thoughts. Then suddenly, the crisis arrived.

The soup and fish courses had been disposed of, and the table was being prepared for the entrée. The host leaned back genially in his chair and said, "By the way, Mr. Burnham, did you know I had an axe to grind in asking you here this evening? That sounds inhospitable, doesn't it? But I'm sure we're all grateful to the axe that has given us the opportunity of meeting you. We are delighted at having discovered you."

Gordon bowed, smiling at the compliment, and the murmurs of hearty assent around the table showed him that he had begun well. If only he could keep it up! But how, *how,* was he to get possession of that magic bit of paper and take it away with him?

"Mr. Burnham, I was delighted to learn through a friend that you are an expert in code-reading. I wonder, did the message that my friend, Mr. Burns sent you this morning give you any information that I wanted you to do me a favor?"

Gordon bowed again. "Yes: it was intimated to me that you had some message you would like deciphered, and I have also sent a letter of introduction from Mr. Burns."

Here Gordon took the letter of introduction from his pocket and handed it across the table to his host, who opened it genially, as if it were hardly necessary to read what was written within since they already knew so delightfully the man whom it introduced. The duplicate cipher writing in Gordon's pocket crackled knowingly when he settled his coat about him again, as if it would say, "My time is coming! It is almost here now."

The young man wondered how he was to get it out without being seen, in case he should want to use it, but he smiled pleasantly at his host with no sign of the perturbation he was feeling.

"You see," went on Mr. Holman, "we have an important message which we cannot read, and our expert who understands all these matters is out of town and cannot return for some time. It is necessary that we know as soon as possible the import of this writing."

While he was speaking Mr. Holman drew from his pocket a long, soft leather wallet and took therefrom a folded paper which Gordon at once recognized as the duplicate of the one he carried in his pocket. His head seemed to reel, and all the lights go dark before him as he reached a cold hand out for the paper. He saw in it his own advancement coming to his eager grasp, yet when he got it would he be able to hold it? Something of the coolness of a man facing a terrible danger came to him now. By sheer force of will he held his trembling fingers steady as he took the bit of paper and opened it carelessly, as if he had never heard of it before, saying as he did so:

"I will do my best."

There was a sudden silence as every eye was fixed upon him while he unfolded the paper. He gave one swift glance about the table before he dropped his eyes to the task. Every face held the intensity of almost terrible eagerness, and on every one but that of the gentle hostess sat cunning — craft that would stop at nothing to serve its own ends. It was a moment of almost awful import.

The next instant Gordon's glance went down to the paper in his hand, and his brain and heart were seized in the grip of fright. There was no other word to describe his feeling. The message before him was clearly written in the code of the home office, and the words stared at him plainly without the necessity of study. The import of them was the revelation of one of the most momentous questions that had to do with the Secret Service work, a question the answer to which had puzzled the entire department for weeks. That answer he now held in his hand, and he knew that if it should come to the knowledge of those outside before it had done its work through the department it would result in dire calamity to the cause of righteousness in the country, and incidentally crush the inefficient messenger who allowed it to become known. For the instant Gordon felt unequal to the task before him. How could he keep these bloodhounds at bay — for such they were, he perceived from the import of the message, bloodhounds who were getting ill-gotten gains from innocent and unsuspecting victims — some of them little children.

But the old chief had picked his man well. Only for an instant the glittering lights darkened before his eyes and the cold perspiration started. Then he rallied his forces and looked up. The welfare of a nation's honor was in his hands, and he would be true. It was a matter of life and death, and he would save it or lose his own life if need be.

He summoned his ready smile.

"I shall be glad to serve you if I can," he said. "Of course I'd like to look this over a few minutes before attempting to read it. Codes are different, you know, from one another, but there is a key to them all if one can just find it out. This looks as if it might be very simple."

The spell of breathlessness was broken. The guests relaxed and went on with their dinner.

Gordon, meanwhile, tried coolly to keep up a pretense of eating, the paper held in one hand while he seemed to be studying it. Once he turned it over and looked on the back.

There was a large crossmark in red ink at the upper end. He looked at it curiously and then instinctively at his host.

"That is my own mark," said Mr. Holman. "I put it there to distinguish it from other papers." He was smiling politely, but he might as well have said, "I put it there to identify it in case of theft;" for every one at the table, unless it might be his wife, understood that that was what he meant. Gordon felt it and was conscious of the other paper in his vest-pocket. The way was going to be difficult.

Among the articles in the envelope which the chief had given him before his departure from Washington were a pair of shell-rimmed eye-glasses, a false mustache, a goatee, and a pair of eyebrows. He had laughed at the suggestion of high-tragedy contained in the disguise, but had brought them with him for a possible emergency. The eye-glasses were tucked into the vest-pocket beside the duplicate paper. He bethought himself of them now. Could he, under cover of taking them out, manage to exchange the papers? And if he should, how about that red-ink mark across the back? Would any one notice its absence? It was well to exchange the papers as soon as possible before the writing had been studied by those at the table, for he knew that the other message, though resembling this one in general words, differed enough to attract the attention of a close observer. Dared he risk their noticing the absence of the red cross on the back?

Slowly, cautiously, under cover of the conversation, he managed to get that duplicate paper out of his pocket and under the napkin in his lap. This he did with one hand, all the time ostentatiously holding the code message in the other hand, with its back to the people at the table. This hand meanwhile also held his coat lapel out that he might the more easily search his vest-pockets for the glasses. It all looked natural. The hostess was engaged in a whispered conversation with the maid at the moment. The host and other guests were finishing the exceedingly delicious patties on their plates, and the precious code message was safely in evidence, red cross and all. They saw no reason to be suspicious about the stranger's hunt for his glasses.

"Oh, here they are!" he said, quite unconcernedly, and put on the glasses to look more closely at the paper, spreading it smoothly on the table cloth before him, and wondering how he should get it into his lap in place of the one that now lay quietly under his napkin.

The host and the guests politely refrained from talking to Gordon and told each other incidents of the day in low tones that indicated the non-importance of what they were saying; while they waited for the real business of the hour.

Then the butler removed the plates, pausing beside Gordon waiting punctiliously with his silver tray to brush away the crumbs.

This was just what Gordon waited for. It had come to him as the only way. Courteously he drew aside, lifting the paper from the table and putting it in his lap, for just the instant while the butler did his work; but in that instant the paper with the red cross was slipped under the napkin, and the other paper took its place upon the table, back down so that its lack of a red cross could not be noted.

So far, so good, but how long could this be kept up? And the paper under the napkin—how was it to be got into his pocket? His hands were like ice now, and his brain seemed to be at boiling heat as he sat back and realized that the deed was done, and could not be undone. If any one should pick up that paper from the table and discover the lack of the red mark, it would be all up with him. He looked up for an instant to meet the gaze of the six men upon him. They had nothing better to do now than to look at him until the next course arrived. He realized that not one of them would have mercy upon him if they knew what he had done, not one unless it might be the tired, old-looking one, and he would not dare interfere.

Still Gordon was enabled to smile, and to say some pleasant nothings to his hostess when she passed him the salted almonds. His hand lay carelessly guarding the secret of the paper on the table, innocently, as though it just *happened* that he laid it on the paper.

Sitting thus with the real paper in his lap under his large damask napkin, the false paper under his hand on the table where he from time to time perused it, and his eye-glasses which made him look most distinguished still on his nose, he heard the distant telephone bell ring.

He remembered the words of his chief and sat rigid. From his position he could see the tall clock in the hall, and its gilded hands pointed to ten minutes before seven. It was about the time his chief had said he would be called on the telephone. What should he do with the two papers?

He had but an instant to think until the well-trained butler returned and announced that some one wished to speak with Mr. Burnham on the telephone. His resolve was taken. He would have to leave the substitute paper on the table. To carry it away with him might arouse suspicion, and, moreover, he could not easily manage both without being noticed. The real paper must be put safely away at all hazards, and he must take the chance that the absence of the red mark would remain unnoticed until his return.

Deliberately he laid a heavy silver spoon across one edge of the paper on the table, and an ice-cream fork across the other, as if to hold it in place until his return. Then, rising with apologies, he gathered his napkin, paper, and all in his hand, holding it against his coat most naturally, as if he had forgotten that he had it, and made his way into the front hall, where in an alcove was the telephone. As he passed the hat-rack he swept his coat and hat off with his free hand, and bore them with him, devoutly hoping that he was not being watched from the dining room. Could he possibly get from the telephone out the front door without being seen? Hastily he hid the cipher message in an inner pocket. The napkin he dropped on the little telephone table, and taking up the receiver he spoke: "Hello! Yes! Oh, good evening! You don't say so! How did that happen?" He made his voice purposely clear, that it might be heard in the dining-room if anyone was listening. Then glancing in that direction saw, to his horror, his host lean over and lift the cipher paper he had left on the table and hand it to the guest on his right.

The messenger at the other end had given his sentence agreed upon and he had replied according to the sentences laid down by the chief in his instructions; the other end had said good-bye and hung up, but Gordon's voice spoke, cool and clear in the little alcove, despite his excitement. "All right. Certainly, I can take time to write it down. Wait until I get my pencil. Now, I'm ready. Have you it there? I'll wait a minute until you get it." His heart beat wildly. The blood surged through his ears like rushing waters. Would they look for the little red mark? The soft clink of spoons and dishes and the murmur of conversation was still going on, but there was no doubt but that it was a matter of few seconds before his theft would be discovered. He must make an instant dash for liberty while he yet could. Cautiously, stealthily, like a shadow from the alcove, one eye on the dining-room, he stole to the door and turned the knob. Yet even as he did so he saw his recent host rise excitedly from his seat and fairly snatch the paper from the man who held it. His last glimpse of the room where he had but three minutes before been enjoying the hospitality of the house was a vision of the entire company starting up and pointing to himself even as he slid from sight. There was no longer need for silence. He had been discovered and must fight for his life. He shut the door quickly, his nerves so tense that it seemed as if something must break soon; opened and slammed the outer door, and was out in the great whirling city under the flare of electric lamps with only the chance of a second of time before his pursuers would be upon him.

He came down the steps with the air of one who could scarcely take time to touch his feet to the ground, but must fly.

3

ALMOST in front of the house stood a closed carriage with two fine horses, but the coachman was looking up anxiously toward the next building. The sound of the closing door drew the man's attention, and, catching Gordon's eye, he made as if to jump down and throw open the door of the carriage. Quick as a flash, Gordon saw he had been mistaken for the man the carriage awaited, and he determined to make use of the circumstance.

"Don't get down," he called to the man, taking chances. "It's very late already. I'll open the door. Drive for all you're worth." He jumped in and slammed the carriage door behind him, and in a second more the horses were flying down the street. A glance from the back window showed an excited group of his fellow-guests standing at the open door of the mansion he had just left pointing toward his carriage and wildly gesticulating. He surmised that his host was already at the telephone calling for his own private detective.

Gordon could scarcely believe his sense that he had accomplished his mission and flight so far, and yet he knew his situation was most precarious. Where he was going he neither knew nor cared. When he was sure he was far enough from the house he would call to the driver and give him directions, but first he must make sure that the precious paper was safely stowed away, in case he should be caught and searched. They might be coming after him with motorcycles in a minute or two.

Carefully rolling the paper into a tiny compass, he slipped it into a hollow gold case which was among the things in the envelope the chief had given him. There was a fine chain attached to the case, and the whole looked innocently like a gold pencil. The chain he slipped about his neck, dropping the case down inside his collar. That done he breathed more freely. Only from his dead body should they take that away. Then he hastily put on the false eyebrows, mustache, and goatee which had been provided for his disguise, and pulling on a pair of light gloves he felt more fit to evade detection.

He was just beginning to think what he should say to the driver about taking him to the station, for it was important that he get out of the city at once, when, glancing out of the window to see what part of the city he was being taken through he became aware of an auto close beside the carriage keeping pace with it, and two men stretching their necks as if to look into the carriage window at him. He withdrew to the shadow instantly so that they could not see him, but the one quick glance he had made him sure that one of his pursuers was the short thick-set man with cruel jaw who had sat across from him at the dinner table a few minutes before. It this were so he had practically no chance at all of escape, for what was a carriage against a swift moving car and what was he against a whole city full of strangers and enemies? If he attempted to drop from the carriage on the other side and escape into the darkness he had but a chance of a thousand at not being seen, and he could not hope to hide and get away in this unknown part of the city. Yet he must take his chance somehow, for the carriage must sooner or later get somewhere and he be obliged to face his pursuers.

To make matters worse, just at the instant when he had

decided to jump at the next dark place and was measuring the distance with his eye, his hand even being outstretched to grasp the door handle, a blustering, boisterous motor-cycle burst into full bloom just where he intended to jump, and the man who rode it was in uniform. He dodged back into the darkness of the carriage again that he might not be seen, and the motor-cycle came so near that its rider turned a white face and looked in. He felt that his time had come, and his cause was lost. It had not yet occurred to him that the men who were pursuing him would hardly be likely to call in municipal aid in their search, lest their own duplicity would be discovered. He reasoned that he was dealing with desperate men who would stop at nothing to get back the original cipher paper, and stop his mouth. He was well aware that only death would be considered a sufficient silencer for him after what he had seen at Mr. Holman's dinner table, for the evidence he could give would involve the honor of every man who had sat there. He saw in a flash that the two henchmen whom he was sure were even now riding in the car on his right had been at the table for the purpose of silencing him if he showed any signs of giving trouble. The wonder was that any of them dared call in a stranger on a matter of such grave import which meant ruin to them all if they were found out, but probably they had reasoned that every man had his price and had intended to offer him a share of the booty. It was likely that the chief had caused it to be understood by them that he was the right kind of man for their purpose. Yet, of course, they had taken precautions, and now they had him well caught, an auto on one side, a motor-cycle on the other and no telling how many more behind! He had been a fool to get into this carriage. He might have known it would only trap him to his death. There seemed absolutely no chance for escape now—yet he must fight to the last. He put his hand on his revolver to make sure it was easy to get at, tried to think whether it would not be better to chew up and swallow that cipher message rather than to run the risk of its falling again into the hands of the enemy; decided that he must carry it intact to his chief if possible; and finally that he must make a dash for safety at once, when just then the carriage turned briskly into a wide driveway, and the attendant auto and motor-cycle dropped behind as if puzzled at the move. The carriage stopped short and a bright light from an open doorway was flung into his face. There seemed to be high stone walls on one side and the lighted doorway on the other hand evidently led into a great stone building. He could hear the puffing of the car and cycle just behind. A wild notion that the carriage had been placed in front of the house to trap him in case he tried to escape, and that he had been brought to prison, flitted through his mind.

His hand was on his revolver as the coachman jumped down to fling open the carriage door, for he intended to fight for his liberty to the last.

He glanced back through the carriage window, and the lights of the auto glared in his face. The short, thick-set man was getting out of the car, and the motor-cyclist had stood his machine up against the wall and was coming toward the carriage. Escape was going to be practically impossible. A wild thought of dashing out the opposite door of his carriage, boldly seizing the motor-cycle and making off on it passed through his mind, and then the door on his left was flung open and the carriage was immediately surrounded by six excited men in evening dress all talking at once. "Here you are at last!" they chorused.

"Where is the best man?" shouted some one from the doorway. "Hasn't he come either?" And as if in answer one of the men by the carriage door wheeled and called excitedly: "Yes, he's come! Tell him—tell Jeff—tell him he's come." Then turning once more to Gordon he seized him by the arm and cried: "Come on quickly! There isn't a minute to wait. The organist is fairly frantic. Everybody has been just as nervous as could be. We couldn't very well go on without you—you know. But don't let that worry you. It's all right now you've come.

Forget it, old man, and hustle." Dimly Gordon perceived above the sound of subdued hubbub that an organ was playing, and even as he listened it burst into the joyous notes of the wedding march. It dawned upon him that this was not a prison to which he had come but a church—not a courtroom but a wedding, and horror of horrors! They took him for the best man. His disguise had been his undoing. How was he to get out of this scrape? And with his pursuers just behind!

"Let me explain—" he began, and wondered what he could explain.

"There's no time for explanations now, man. I tell you the organ has begun the march. We're expected to be marching down that middle aisle this very minute and Jeff is waiting for us in the chapel. I sent the signal to the bride and another to the organist the minute we sighted you. Come on! Everybody knows your boat was late in coming in. You don't need to explain a thing till afterwards."

At the moment one of the ushers moved aside and the short, thick-set man stepped between, the light shining full upon his face, and Gordon knew him positively for the man who had sat opposite him at the table a few minutes before. He was peering eagerly into the carriage door and Gordon saw his only escape was into the church. With his heart pounding like a trip hammer he yielded himself to the six ushers, who swept the little pursuer aside as if he had been a fly and literally bore Gordon up the steps and into the church door.

A burst of music filled his senses, and dazzling lights, glimpses of flowers, palms and beautiful garments bewildered him. His one thought was for escape from his pursuers. Would they follow him into the church and drag him out in the presence of all these people, or would they be thrown off the track for a little while and give him opportunity yet to get away? He looked around wildly for a place of exit but he was in the hands of the insistent ushers. One of them chattered to him in a low, growling whisper, such as men use on solemn occasions:

"It must have been rough on you being anxious like this about getting here, but never mind now. It'll go all right. Come on. Here's our cue and there stands Jefferson over there. You and he go in with the minister, you know. The groom and the best man, you understand, they'll tell you when. Jeff has the ring all right, so you won't need to bother about that. There's absolutely nothing for you to do but stand where you're put and go out when the rest do. You needn't feel a bit nervous."

Was it possible that these crazy people didn't recognize their mistake even yet here in the bright light? Couldn't they see his mustache was stuck on and one eyebrow was crooked? Didn't they know their best man well enough to recognize his voice? Surely, surely, some one would discover the mistake soon — that man Jeff over there who was eyeing him so intently. He would be sure to know this was not his friend. Yet every minute that they continued to think so was a distinct gain for Gordon, puzzling his pursuers and giving himself time to think and plan and study his strange surroundings.

And now they were drawing him forward and a turn of his head gave him a vision of the stubbed head of the thickset man peering in at the chapel door and watching him eagerly. He must fool him if possible.

"But I don't know anything about the arrangements," faltered Gordon, reflecting that the best man might not be very well known to the ushers and perhaps he resembled him. It was not the first time he had been taken for another man — and with his present make-up and all, perhaps it was natural. Could he possibly hope to bluff it out for a few minutes until the ceremony was over and then escape? It would of course be the best way imaginable to throw that impudent little man in the doorway off his track. If the real best man would only stay away long enough it would not be a difficult part to play. The original man might turn up after he was gone and create a pleasant little mystery, but nobody would be injured thereby. All this passed through his mind while the usher kept up his sepulchral whisper:

"Why, there are just the usual arrangements, you know — nothing new. You and Jeff go in after the ushers have reached the back of the church and opened the door. Then you just stand there till Celia and her uncle come up the aisle. Then follows the ceremony — very brief. Celia had all that repeating after the minister cut out on account of not being able to rehearse. It's to be just the simplest service, not the usual lengthy affair. Don't worry, you'll be all right, old man. Hurry! They're calling you. Leave your hat right here. Now I must go. Keep cool. It'll soon be over."

The breathless usher hurried through the door and settled into a sort of exalted hobble to the time of the wonderful Lohengrin music. Gordon turned, thinking even yet to make a possible escape, but the eagle-eye of his pursuer was upon him and the man Jefferson was by his side:

"Here we are!" he said, eagerly grabbing Gordon's hat and coat and dumping them on a chair. "I'll look after everything. Just come along. It's time we went in. The doctor is motioning for us. Awfully glad to see you at last. Too bad you had to rush so. How many years is it since I saw you? Ten! You've changed some, but you're looking fine and dandy. No need to worry about anything. It'll soon be over and the knot tied."

Mechanically Gordon fell into place beside the man Jefferson, who was a pleasant-faced youth, well-groomed and handsome. Looking furtively at his finely-cut, happy features, Gordon wondered if he would feel as glad as this youth seemed to be, when he walked down the aisle to meet his bride. How, by the way, would he feel if were going to be married now, — going into the face of this great company of well-dressed people to meet Miss Julia Bentley and be joined to her for life? Instinctively his soul shrank within him at the thought.

But now the door was wide open, the organ pealing its best, and he suddenly became aware of many eyes, and of wondering how long his eyebrows would withstand the perspiration that was trickling softly down his forehead. His mustache — ridiculous appendage! why had he not removed it? — was it awry? Dared he put up his hand to see? His gloves! Would any one notice that they were not as strictly fresh as a best man's gloves should be? Then he took his first step to the music, and it was like being pulled from a delicious morning nap and plunged into a tub of icy water.

He walked with feet that suddenly weighed like lead, across a church that looked to be miles in width, in the face of swarms of curious eyes. He tried to reflect that these people were all strangers to him, that they were not looking at him, any way, but at the bridegroom by his side, and that it mattered very little what he did, so long as he kept still and braved it out, if only the real best man didn't turn up until he was well out of the church. Then he could vanish in the dark, and go by some back way to a car or a taxicab and so to the station. The thought of the paper inside the gold pencil-case filled him with a sort of elation. If only he could get out of this dreadful church, he would probably get away safely. Perhaps even the incident of the wedding might prove to be his protection, for they would never seek him in a crowded church at a fashionable wedding.

The man by his side managed him admirably, giving him a whispered hint, a shove, or a push now and then, and getting him into the proper position. It seemed as if the best man had to occupy the most trying spot in all the church, but as they put him there, of course it was right. He glanced furtively over the faces near the front, and they all looked quite satisfied, as if everything were going as it should, so he settled down to his fate, his white, strained face partly hidden by the abundant display of mustache and eyebrow. People whispered softly how handsome he looked, and some suggested that he was not so stout as when they had last seen him, ten years before. His stay in a foreign land must have done him good. One woman went so far as to tell her daughter that he was far more distinguished-looking than she had ever thought he could become, but it was wonderful what a stay in a foreign land would do to improve a person.

The music stole onward; and slowly, gracefully, like the opening of buds into flowers, the bridal party inched along up the middle aisle until at last the bride in all the mystery of her white veil arrived, and all the maidens in their flowers and many colored gauzes were suitably disposed about her.

The feeble old man on whose arm the bride had leaned as she came up the aisle dropped out of the procession, melting into one of the front seats, and Gordon found himself standing beside the bride. He felt sure there must be something wrong about it, and looked at his young guide with an attempt to change places with him, but the man named Jefferson held him in place with a warning eye. "You're all right. Just stay where you are," he whispered softly, and Gordon stayed, reflecting on the strange fashions of weddings, and wondering why he had never before taken notice of just how a wedding party came in and stood and got out again. If he was only out of this how glad he would be. It seemed one had to be a pretty all-around man to be a member of the Secret Service.

The organ had hushed its voice to a sort of exultant sobbing, filled with dreams of flowers and joys, and hints of sorrow; and the minister in a voice both impressive and musical began the ceremony. Gordon stood doggedly and wondered if that really was one eyebrow coming down over his eye, or only a drop of perspiration.

Another full second passed, and he decided that if he ever got out of this situation alive he would never, no, never, *no never,* get married himself.

During the next second that crawled by he became supremely conscious of the creature in white by his side. A desire possessed him to look at her and see if she were like

Julia Bentley. It was like a nightmare haunting his dreams that she *was* Julia Bentley somehow transported to New York and being married to him willy-nilly. He could not shake it off, and the other eyebrow began to feel shaky. He was sure it was sailing down over his eye. If he only dared press its adhesive lining a little tighter to his flesh!

Some time during the situation there came a prayer, interminable to his excited imagination, as all the other ceremonies.

Under cover of the hush and the supposedly bowed heads, Gordon turned desperately toward the bride. He must see her and drive this phantasm from his brain. He turned, half expecting to see Julia's tall, handsome form, though telling himself he was a fool, and wondering why he so dreaded the idea. Then his gaze was held fascinated.

She was a little creature, slender and young and very beautiful, with a beauty which a deathly pallor only enhanced. Her face was delicately cut, and set in a frame of fine dark hair, the whole made most exquisite by the mist of white tulle that breathed itself about her like real mist over a flower. But the lovely head drooped, the coral lips had a look of unutterable sadness, and the long lashes swept over white cheeks. He could not take his eyes from her now that he had looked. How lovely, and how fitting for the delightful youth by his side! Now that he thought of it she was like him, only smaller and more delicate, of course. A sudden fierce, ridiculous feeling of envy filled Gordon's heart. Why couldn't he have known and loved a girl like that? Why had Julia Bentley been forever in his pathway as the girl laid out for his choice?

He looked at her with such intensity that a couple of dear old sisters who listened to the prayer with their eyes wide open, whispered one to the other: "Just see him look at her! How he must love her! Wasn't it beautiful that he should come right from the steamer to the church and never see her till now, for the first time in ten long years. It's so romantic!"

"Yes," whispered the other; "and I believe it'll last. He looks at her that way. Only I do dislike that way of arranging the hair on his face. But then it's foreign I suppose. He'll probably get over it if they stay in this country."

A severe old lady in the seat in front turned a reprimanding chin toward them and they subsided. Still Gordon continued to gaze.

Then the bride became aware of his look, raised her eyes, and—they were full of tears!

They gave him one reproachful glance that shot through his soul like a sword, and her lashes drooped again. By some mysterious control over the law of gravity, the tears remained unshed, and the man's gaze was turned aside; but that look had done its mighty work.

All the experiences of the day rushed over him and seemed to culminate in that one look. It was as if the reproach of all things had come upon him. The hurt in the white dog's eyes had touched him, the perfect courage in the appeal of the child's eyes had called forth his deepest sympathy, but the tears of this exquisite woman wrung his heart. He saw now that the appeal of the dog and the child had been the opening wedge for the look of a woman which tore self from him and flung it at her feet for her to walk upon; and when the prayer was ended he found that he was trembling.

He looked vindictively at the innocent youth beside him, as the soft rustle of the audience and the little breath of relief from the bridal party betokened the next stage in the ceremony. What had this innocent-looking youth done to cause tears in those lovely eyes? Was she marrying him against her will? He was only a boy, any way. What right had he to suppose he could care for a delicate creature like that? He was making her cry already, and he seemed to be utterly unconscious of it. What could be the matter? Gordon felt a desire to kick him.

Then it occurred to him that inadvertently *he* might have been the cause of her tears; he, supposedly the best man, who had been late, and held up the wedding no knowing how long. Of course it wasn't really his fault; but by proxy it was, for he now was masquerading as that unlucky best man, and she was very likely reproaching him for what she supposed was his stupidity. He had heard that women cried sometimes from vexation, disappointment or excitement.

Yet in his heart of hearts he could not set those tears, that look, down to so trivial a cause. They had reached his very soul, and he felt there was something deeper there than mere vexation. There had been bitter reproach for a deep wrong done. The glance had told him that. All the manhood in him rose to defend her against whoever had hurt her. He longed to get one more look into her eyes to make quite sure; and then, if there was still appeal there, his soul must answer it.

For the moment his commission, his ridiculous situation, the real peril to his life and trust, were forgotten.

The man Jefferson had produced a ring and was nudging him. It appeared that the best man had some part to play with that ring. He dimly remembered somewhere hearing that the best man must hand the ring to the bridegroom at the proper moment, but it was absurd for them to go through the farce of doing that when the bridegroom already held the golden circlet in his fingers! Why did he not step up like a man and put it upon the outstretched hand; that little white hand just in front of him there, so timidly held out with its glove fingers tucked back, like a dove crept out from its covert unwillingly?

But that Jefferson-man still held out the ring stupidly to him, and evidently expected him to take it. Silly youth! There was nothing for it but to take it and hand it back, of course. He must do as he was told and hasten that awful ceremony to its interminable close. He took the ring and held it out, but the young man did not take it again. Instead he whispered, "Put it on her finger!"

Gordon frowned. Could he be hearing aright? Why didn't

the fellow put the ring on his own bride? If he were being married, he would knock any man down that dared to put his wife's wedding ring on for him. Could that be the silly custom now, to have the best man put the bride's ring on? How unutterably out of place! But he must not make a scene, of course.

The little timid hand, so slender and white, came a shade nearer as if to help, and the ring finger separated itself from the others.

He looked at the smooth circlet. It seemed too tiny for any woman's finger. Then, reverently, he slipped it on, with a strange, inexpressible longing to touch the little hand. While he was thinking himself all kinds of a fool, and was enjoying one of his intermittent visions of Julia Bentley's expressive countenance interpolated on the present scene, a strange thing happened.

There had been some low murmurs and motions which he had not noticed because he thought his part of this very uncomfortable affair was about concluded, when, lo and behold, the minister and the young man by his side both began fumbling for his hand, and among them they managed to bring it into position and place in its astonished grasp the little timid hand that he had just crowned with its ring.

As his fingers closed over the bride's hand, there was such reverence, such tenderness in his touch that the girl's eyes were raised once more to his face, this time with the conquered tears in retreat, but all the pain and appeal still there. He looked and involuntarily he pressed her hand the closer, as if to promise aforetime whatever she would ask. Then, with her hand in his, and with the realization that they two were detached as it were from the rest of the wedding party, standing in a little centre of their own, his senses came back to him, and he perceived as in a flash of understanding that it was *they* who were being married!

There had been some terrible, unexplainable mistake, and he was stupidly standing in another man's place, taking vows upon himself! The thing had passed from an adventure of little moment into the matter of a life-tragedy, two life-tragedies perhaps! What should he do?

With the question came the words, "I pronounce you husband and wife," and "let no man put asunder."

4

WHAT had he done? Was it some great unnamed, unheard-of crime he had unconsciously committed? Could any one understand or excuse such asinine stupidity? Could he ever hold up his head again, though he fled to the most distant part of the globe? Was there nothing that could save the situation? Now, before they left the church, could he not declare the truth, and set things right, undo the words that had been spoken in the presence of all these witnesses, and send out to find the real bridegroom? Surely neither law nor gospel could endorse a bond made in the ignorance of either participant. It would, of course, be a terrible thing for the bride, but better now than later. Besides, he was pledged by that hand-clasp to answer the appeal in her eyes and protect her. This, then, was what it had meant!

But his commission! What of that? "A matter of life and death!" Ah! but this was *more* than life or death!

While these rapid thoughts were flashing through his brain, the benediction was being pronounced, and with the last word the organ pealed forth its triumphant lay. The audience stirred excitedly, anticipating the final view of the wedding procession.

The bride turned to take her bouquet from the maid of honor, and the movement broke the spell under which Gordon had been held.

He turned to the young man by his side and spoke hurriedly in a low tone.

"An awful mistake has been made," he said, and the organ drowned everything but the word "mistake." "I don't know what to do," he went on. But young Jefferson hastened to reassure him joyously:

"Not a bit of it, old chap. Nobody noticed that hitch about the ring. It was only a second. Everything went off slick. You haven't anything more to do now but take my sister out. Look alive, there! She looks as if she might be going to faint! She hasn't been a bit well all day! Steady her, quick, can't you? She'll stick it out till she gets to the air, but hurry, for goodness' sake!"

Gordon turned in alarm. Already the frail white bride had a claim on him. His first duty was to get her out of this crowd. Perhaps, after all, she had discovered that he was not the right man, and that was the meaning of her tears and appeal. Yet she had held her own and allowed things to go through to the finish, and perhaps he had no right to reveal to the assembled multitudes what she evidently wanted kept quiet. He must wait till he could ask her. He must do as this other man said — this — this brother of hers — who was of course the best man. Oh fool, and blind! Why had he not understood at the beginning and got himself out of this fix before it was too late? And what should he do when he reached the door? How could he ever explain? His commission! He dared not breathe a word of that! What explanation could he possibly offer for his — his — yes — his *criminal* conduct? Why, no such thing was ever heard of in the history of mankind as that which had happened to him. From start to finish it was — it — was — He could not think of words to express what it was.

He was by this time meandering jerkily down the aisle,

attempting to keep time to the music and look the part that she evidently expected him to play, but his eyes were upon her face, which was whiter now and, if possible, lovelier, than before.

"Oh, just see how devoted he is," murmured the eldest of the two dear old sisters, and he caught the sense of her words as he passed, and wondered. Then, immediately before him, retreating backward down the aisle with terrible eyes of scorn upon him he seemed to feel the presence of Miss Julia Bentley leading onward toward the church door; but he would not take his eyes from that sweet, sad face of the white bride on his arm to look. He somehow knew that if he could hold out until he reached that door without looking up, her power over him would be exorcised forever.

Out into the vacant vestibule, under the tented canopy, alone together for the moment, he felt her gentle weight grow heavy on his arm, and knew her footsteps were lagging. Instinctively, lest others should gather around them, he almost lifted her and bore her down the carpeted steps, through the covered pathway, to the luxurious motor-car waiting with open door, and placed her on the cushions. Some one closed the car door and almost immediately they were in motion.

She settled back with a half sigh, as if she could not have borne one instant more of strain, then sitting opposite he adjusted the window to give her air. She seemed grateful but said nothing. Her eyes were closed wearily, and the whole droop of her figure showed utter exhaustion. It seemed a desecration to speak to her, yet he must have some kind of an understanding before they reached their destination.

"An explanation is due to you—" he began, without knowing just what he was going to say, but she put out her hand with a weary protest.

"Oh, please don't!" she pleaded. "I know—the boat was late! It doesn't matter in the least."

He sat back appalled! She did not herself know then that she had married the wrong man!

"But you don't understand," he protested.

"Never mind," she moaned. "I don't want to understand. Nothing can change things. Only, let me be quiet till we get to the house, or I never can go through with the rest of it."

Her words ended with almost a sob, and he sat silent for an instant, with a mingling of emotions, uppermost of which was a desire to take the little, white, shrinking girl into his arms and comfort her, "Nothing can change things!" That sounded as though she did know but thought it too late to undo the great mistake now that it had been made. He must let her know that he had not understood until the ceremony was over. While he sat helplessly looking at her in the dimness of the car where she looked so small and sad and misty huddled beside her great bouquet, she opened her eyes and looked at him. She seemed to understand that he was about to speak again. By the great arc light they were passing he saw there were tears in her eyes again, and her voice held a child-like pleading as she uttered one word:

"Don't!"

It hurt him like a knife, he knew not why. But he could not resist the appeal. Duty or no duty, he could not disobey her command.

"Very well." He said it quietly, almost tenderly, and sat back with folded arms. After all, what explanation could he give her that she would believe? He might not breathe a word of his commission or the message. What other reason could he give for his extraordinary appearance at her wedding and by her side?

The promise in his voice seemed to give her relief. She breathed a sigh of relief and closed her eyes. He must just keep still and have his eyes open for a chance to escape when the carriage reached its destination.

Thus silently they threaded through unknown streets,

strange thoughts in the heart of each. The bride was struggling with her heavy burden, and the man was trying to think his way out of the maze of perplexity into which he had unwittingly wandered. He tried to set his thoughts in order and find out just what to do. First of all, of course came his commission, but somehow every time the little white bride opposite took first place in his mind. Could he serve both? What *would* serve both, and what would serve *either?* As for himself, he was free to confess that there was no room left in the present situation for even a consideration of his own interests.

Whatever there was of good in him must go now to set matters right in which he had greatly blundered. He must do the best he could for the girl who had so strangely crossed his pathway, and get back to his commission. But when he tried to realize the importance of his commission and set it over against the interests of the girl-bride, his mind became confused. What should he do? He could not think of slipping away and leaving her without further words, even if an opportunity offered itself. Perhaps he was wrong. Doubtless his many friends might tell him so if they were consulted, but he did not intend to consult them. He intended to see this troubled soul to some place of safety, and look out for his commission as best he could afterward. One thing he did not fully realize, and that was that Miss Julia Bentley's vision troubled him no longer. He was free. There was only one woman in the whole wide world that gave him any concern, and that was the little sorrowful creature who sat opposite to him, and to whom he had just been married.

Just been married! He! The thought brought with it a thrill of wonder, and a something else that was not unpleasant. What if he really had? Of course he had not. Of course such a thing could not hold good. But what if he had? Just for an instant he entertained the thought — would he be glad or sorry? He did not know her of course, had heard her speak but a few words, had looked into her face plainly but once, and yet suppose she were his! His heart answered the question with a glad bound and astonished him, and all his former ideas of real love were swept from his mind in a breath. He knew that, stranger though she was, he could take her to his heart; cherish her, love her and bear with her, as he never could have done Julia Bentley. Then all at once he realized that he was allowing his thoughts to dwell upon a woman who by all that was holy belonged to another man, and that other man would doubtless soon be the one with whom he would have to deal. He would soon be face to face with a new phase of the situation and he must prepare himself to meet it. What was he going to do? Should he plan to escape from the opposite door of the automobile while the bride was being assisted from her seat? No, he could not, for he would be expected to get out first and help her out. Besides, there would be too many around, and he could not possibly get away. But, greater than any such reason, the thing that held him bound was the look in her eyes through the tears. He simply could not leave her until he knew that she no longer needed him. And yet there was his commission! Well, he must see her in the hands of those who would care for her at least. So much he had done even for the white dog, and then, too, surely she was worth as many minutes of his time as he had been compelled to give to the injured child of the streets. If he only could explain to her now!

The thought of his message, with its terrible significance, safe in his possession, sent shivers of anxiety through his frame! Suppose he should be caught, and it taken from him, all on account of this most impossible incident! What scorn, what contumely, would be his! How could he ever explain to his chief? Would anybody living believe that a man in his senses could be married to a stranger before a whole church full of people and not know he was being married until the deed was done — and then not do anything about it after it was done? That was what he was doing now this very minute. He ought to be explaining something somehow to that poor little creature in the shadow of the carriage. Perhaps in some way it might relieve her sorrow if he did, and yet when he looked at her and tried to speak his mouth was hopelessly closed. He might not tell her anything!!

He gradually sifted his immediate actions down to two necessities; to get his companion to a safe place where her friends could care for her, and to make his escape as soon and as swiftly as possible. It was awful to run and leave her without telling her anything about it; when she evidently believed him to be the man she had promised and intended to marry; but the real bridegroom would surely turn up soon somehow and make matters right. Anyhow, it was the least he could do to take himself out of her way and to get his trust to its owners at once.

The car halted suddenly before a brightly lighted mansion, whose tented entrance effectually shut out the gaze of alien eyes, and made the transit from car to domicile entirely private. There was no opportunity here to disappear. The sidewalk and road were black with curious onlookers. He stepped from the car first and helped the lady out. He bore her heavy bouquet because she looked literally too frail to carry it further herself.

In the doorway she was surrounded by a bevy of servants, foremost among whom her old nurse claimed the privilege of greeting her with tears and smiles and many "Miss-Celia-my-dears," and Gordon stood for the instant entranced, watching the sweet play of loving kindness in the face of the pale little bride. As soon as he could lay down those flowers inconspicuously he would be on the alert for a way of escape. It surely would be found through some back or side entrance of the house.

But even as the thought came to him the old nurse stepped back to let the other servants greet the bride with stiff bows and embarrassed words of blessing, and he felt a hand laid heavily on his arm.

He started as he turned, thinking instantly again of his

commission and expecting to see a policeman in uniform by his side, but it was only the old nurse, with tears of devotion still in her faded eyes.

"Mister George, ye hevn't forgot me, hev ye?" she asked, earnestly. "You usen't to like me verra well, I mind, but ye was awful for the teasin' an' I was always for my Miss Celie! But bygones is bygones now an' I wish ye well. Yer growed a man, an' I know ye must be worthy o' her, or she'd never hev consented to take ye. Yev got a gude wife an' no mistake, an' I know ye'll be the happiest man alive. Ye won't hold it against me, Mister George, that I used to tell yer uncle on your masterful tricks, will ye? You mind I was only carin' fer my baby girl, an' ye were but a boy."

She paused as if expecting an answer, and Gordon embbarrassedly assured her that he would never think of holding so trifling a matter against her. He cast a look of reverent admiration and tenderness toward the beautiful girl who was smiling on her loyal subjects like a queen, roused from her sorrow to give joy to others; and even her old nurse was satisfied.

"Ah, ye luve her, Mister George, don't ye?" the nurse questioned. "I don't wonder. Everybody what lays eyes on her luves her. She's that dear—" here the tears got the better of the good woman for an instant and she forgot herself and pulled at the skirt of her new black dress thinking it was an apron, and wishing to wipe her eyes.

Then suddenly Gordon found his lips uttering strange words, without his own apparent consent, as if his heart had suddenly taken things in hand and determined to do as it pleased without consulting his judgment.

"Yes, I love her," he was saying, and to his amazement he found that the words were true.

This discovery made matters still more complicated.

"Then ye'll promise me something, Mister George, won't ye?" said the nurse eagerly, her tears having their own way down her rosy anxious face. "Ye'll promise me never to make

her feel bad any more? She's cried a lot these last three months
an' nobody knows but me. She could hide it from them all
but her old nurse that has loved her so long. But she's been
that sorrowful, enough fer a whole lifetime. Promise that ye'l
do all in yer power to make her happy always."

"I will do all in my power to make her happy," he said
solemnly, as if he were uttering a vow, and wondered how
short-lived that power was to be.

5

THE wedding party had arrived in full force now. Carriages and automobiles were unloading; gay voices and laughter filled the house. The servants disappeared to their places, and the white bride, with only a motioning look toward Gordon, led the way to the place where they were to stand under an arch of roses, lilies and palms, in a room hung from the ceiling with drooping ferns and white carnations on invisible threads of silver wire, until it all seemed like a fairy dream.

Gordon had no choice but to follow, as his way was blocked by the incoming guests, and he foresaw that his exit would have to be made from some other door than the front if he were to escape yet awhile. As he stepped into the mystery of the flower-scented room where his lady led the way, he was conscious of a feeling of transition from the world of ordinary things into one of wonder, beauty and mysterious joy; but all the time he knew he was an imposter, who had no right in that silver-threaded bower.

Yet there he stood bowing, shaking hands, and smirking behind his false mustache, which threatened every minute to betray him.

People told him he was looking well, and congratulated him on his bride. Some said he was stouter than when he left the country, and some said he was thinner. They asked him questions about relatives and friends living and dead, and he ran constant risk of getting into hopeless difficulties. His only safety was in smiling, and saying very little; seeming not to hear some questions, and answering others with another question. It was not so hard after he got started, because there were so many people, and they kept coming close upon one another, so no one had much time to talk. Then supper with its formalities was got through with somehow, though to Gordon, with his already satisfied appetite and his hampering mustache, it seemed an endless ordeal.

"Jeff," as they called him, was everywhere, attending to everything, and he slipped up to the unwilling bridegroom just as he was having to answer a very difficult question about the lateness of his vessel, and the kind of passage they had experienced in crossing. By this time Gordon had discovered that he was supposed to have been ten years abroad, and his steamer had been late in landing, but where he came from or what he had been doing over there were still to be found out; and it was extremely puzzling to be asked from what port he had sailed, and how he came to be there when he had been supposed to have been in St. Petersburg but the week before? His state of mind was anything but enviable. Beside all this, Gordon was just reflecting that the last he had seen of his hat and coat was in the church. What had become of them, and how could he go to the station without a hat? Then opportunely "Jeff" arrived.

"Your train leaves at ten three," he said in a low, business-like tone, as if he enjoyed the importance of having made all the arrangements. "I've secured the stateroom as you cabled me to do, and here are the tickets and checks. The trunks are down there all checked. Celia didn't want any nonsense about their being tied up with white ribbon. She hates all that. We've arranged for you to slip out by the fire-escape and down through the back yard of the next neighbor, where a motor, just a plain regular one from the station, will be waiting around the corner in the shadow. Celia knows where it is. None of the party will know you are gone until you are well under way. The car they think you will take is being elaborately adorned with white at the front door now, but you won't have any trouble about it. I've fixed everything up. Your coat and hat are out on the fire-escape, and as soon as Celia's ready I'll show you the way."

Gordon thanked him. There was nothing else to do, but his countenance grew blank. Was there, then, to be no escape? Must he actually take another man's bride with him in order to get away? And how was he to get away from her? Where was the real bridegroom and why did he not appear upon that scene? And yet what complications that might bring up. He began to look wildly about for a chance to flee at once, for how could he possibly run away with a bride on his hands? If only someone were going with them to the station he could slip away with a clear conscience, leaving her in good hands, but to leave her alone, ill and distressed was out of the question. He had rid himself of a lonely dog and a suffering child, though it gave him anguish to do the deed, but leave this lovely woman for whom he at least appeared to have become responsible, he could not, until he was sure she would come to no harm through him.

"Don't let anything hinder you! Don't let anything hinder you!"

It appeared that this refrain had not ceased for an instant since it began, but had chimed its changes through music, ceremony, prayer and reception without interruption. It acted like a goad upon his conscience now. He must do something that would set him free to go back to Washington. An inspiration came to him.

"Wouldn't you like to go to the station with us?" he asked the young man. "I am sure your sister would like to have you."

The boy's face lit up joyfully.

"Oh, wouldn't you mind? I'd like it awfully, and—if it's all the same to you, I wish Mother could go too. It's the first time Celia and she were ever separated, and I know she hates it fiercely to have to say good-by with the house full of folks this way. But she doesn't expect it of course, and really it isn't fair to you, when you haven't seen Celia alone yet, and it's your wedding trip—"

"There will be plenty of time for us," said the compulsory bridegroom graciously, and felt as if he had perjured himself. It was not in his nature to enjoy a serious masquerade of this kind.

"I shall be glad to have you both come," he added earnestly. "I really want you. Tell your mother."

The boy grasped his hand impulsively:

"I say," said he, "you're all right! I don't mind confessing that I've hated the very thought of you for a whole three months, ever since Celia told us she had promised to marry you. You see, I never really knew you when I was a little chap, but I didn't used to like you. I took an awful scunner to you for some reason. I suppose kids often take irrational dislikes like that. But ever since I've laid eyes on you to-night, I've liked you all the way through. I like your eyes. It isn't a bit as I thought I remembered you. I used to think your eyes had a sort of deceitful look. Awful to tell you, isn't it? But I felt as if I wanted to have it off my conscience, for I see now you're nothing of the kind. You've got the honestest eyes I ever saw on a man, and I'd stake my last cent that you wouldn't cheat a church mouse. You're true as steel, and I'm mighty glad you're my brother-in-law. I know you'll be good to Celia."

The slow color mounted under his disguise until it reached Gordon's burnished brown hair. His eyes *were* honest eyes. They had always been so—until to-day. Into what a world of deceit he had entered! How he would like to make a clean breast of it all to this nice, frank boy; but he must not! for there was his trust! For an instant he was on the point of trying to explain that he was not the true bridegroom, and getting young Jefferson to help him to set matters right, but an influx of newly arrived guests broke in upon their privacy, and he could only press the boy's hand and say in embarrassed tones:

"Thank you! I shall try to be worthy of your good opinion hereafter!"

It was over at least, and the bride slipped from his side to prepare for the journey. He looked hastily around, feeling that his very first opportunity had come for making an escape. If an open window had presented itself, he would have vaulted through, trusting to luck and his heels to get away, but there was no window, and every door was blocked by staring, admiring, smirking people. He bethought himself of the fire escape where waited his hat and coat, and wondered if he could find it.

With smiling apologies, he broke away from those around him, murmuring something about being needed, and worked his way firmly but steadily toward the stairs and thence to the back halls. Coming at last upon an open window, he slipped through, his heart beating wildly. He thought for a second that he was there ahead of the others; but a dark form loomed ahead and he perceived some one coming up from outside. Another second, and he saw it was his newly acquired brother-in-law.

"Say, this is great!" was his greeting. "How did you manage to find your way up alone? I was just coming down after you. I wanted to leave you there till the last minute so no one would suspect, but now you are here we can hustle off at once. I just took Mother and Celia down. It was pretty stiff for Mother to climb down, for she was a little bit afraid, but she was game all right, and she was so pleased to go. They're waiting for us down there in the court. Here, let me help you with your overcoat. Now I'll pull down this window, so no one will suspect us and follow. That's all right now, come on! You go ahead. Just hold on to the railing and go slow. I'll keep close to you. I know the way in my sleep. I've played fire here many a year, and could climb down in my sleep."

Gordon found himself wishing that this delightful brother-in-law were really his. There was evidently to be no opportunity of escape here. He meditated making a dash and getting away in the dark when they should reach the foot of the stairs; much as he hated to leave that way, he felt he must do so if there was any chance for him at all; but when they reached the ground he saw that was hopeless. The car that was to take them to the station was drawn up close to the spot, and the chauffeur stood beside it.

"Your mother says fer you to hurry, Mister Jefferson," he called in a sepulchral tone. "They're coming out around the block to watch. Get in as quick as you can."

The burly chauffeur stood below Gordon, helped him to alight on his feet from the fire-escape, and hustled him into the darkness of the conveyance.

They were very quiet until they had left in the dark court and were speeding away down the avenue. Then the bride's mother laid two gentle hands upon Gordon's, leaning across from her seat to do so, and said:

"My son, I shall never forget this of you, never! It was dear of you to give me this last few minutes with my darling!"

Gordon, deeply touched and much put to it for words, mumbled something about being very glad to have her, and Jefferson relieved the situation by pouring forth a volume of information and questions, fortunately not pausing long enough to have the latter answered. The bride sat with one hand clasped in her mother's, and said not a word. Gordon was haunted by the thought of tears in her eyes.

There was little opportunity for thinking, but Gordon made a hasty plan. He decided to get his party all out to the train and then remember his suitcase, which he had left checked in the station. Jefferson would probably insist upon going for it but he would insist more strenuously that the brother and sister would want to have this last minute together. Then he could get away in the crowd and disappear, coming later for his suit-case perhaps, or sending a porter from his own train for it. The only drawback to this arrangement was that it seemed a dishonorable way to leave these people who would in the nature of things be left in a most trying position by his disappearance, especially the sad little bride. But it could not be helped, and his staying would only complicate things still further, for he would have to explain who he was, and that was practically impossible on account of his commission. It would not do to run risks with himself until his mission was accomplished and his message delivered. After that he could confess and make whatever reparation a man in his strange position could render.

The plan worked very well. The brother of course eagerly urged that he be allowed to go back for the suit-case, but Gordon, with well-feigned thoughtfulness, said in a low tone:

"Your sister will want you for a minute all to herself."

A tender look came into the boy's eyes, and he turned back smiling to the stateroom where his mother and sister were having a wordless farewell. Gordon jumped from the train and sprinted down the platform, feeling meaner than he ever remembered to have felt in his whole life, and with a strange heaviness about his heart. He forgot for the moment that there was need for him to be on his guard against possible detectives sent by Mr. Holman. Even the importance of the message he carried seemed to weigh less, now that he was free. His feet had a strange unwillingness to hurry, and without a constant pressure of the will would have lagged in spite of him. His heart wanted to let suit-case and commission and everything else go to the winds and take him back to the state-room where he had left his sorrowful bride of an hour. She was not his, and he might not go, but he knew that he would never be the same hereafter. He would always be wondering where she was, wishing he could have saved her from whatever troubled her; wishing she were his bride, and not another's.

He passed back through the station gate, and a man in evening clothes eyed him sharply. He fancied he saw a resemblance to one of the men at the Holman dinner-table, but he dared not look again lest a glance should cost him recognition. He wondered blindly which way he should take, and if it would be safe to risk going at once to the checking window, or whether he ought to go in hiding until he was sure young Jefferson would no longer look for him. Then a hand touched his shoulder and a voice that was strangely welcome shouted:

"This way, George! The checking place is over to the right!"

He turned and there stood Jefferson, smiling and panting:

"You see, the little mother had something to say to Celia alone, so I saw I was *de trop,* and I thought I better come with you," he declared as soon as he could get his breath.

"Gee, but you can run!" added the panting youth. "What's the hurry? It's ten whole minutes before the train leaves. I couldn't waste all that time kicking my heels on the platform, when I might be enjoying my new brother-in-law's company. I say, are you really going to live permanently in Chicago? I do wish you'd decide to come back to New York. Mother'll miss Celia no end. I don't know how she's going to stand it."

Walking airily by Gordon's side, he talked, apparently not noticing the sudden start and look of mingled anxiety and relief that overspread his brother-in-law's countenance. Then another man walked by them and turning looked in their faces. Gordon was sure this was the thick-set man from Holman's. He was eyeing Gordon keenly. Suddenly all other questions stepped into the backgrond, and the only immediate matter that concerned him was his message, to get it safely to its destination. With real relief he saw that this had been his greatest concern all the time, underneath all hindrances, and that there had not been at any moment any escape from the crowding circumstances other than that he had taken, step by step. If he had been beset by thieves and blackguards, and thrown into prison for a time he would not have felt shame at the delay, for those things he could not help. He saw with new illumination that there was no more shame to him from these trivial and peculiar circumstances with which he had been hemmed in since his start to New York than if he had been checked by any more tragic obstacles. His only real misgiving was about his marriage. Somehow it seemed his fault, and he felt there ought to be some way to confess his part at once — but how — without putting his message in jeopardy — for no one would believe unless they knew all.

But the time of danger was at hand, he plainly saw. The man whom he dared not look closely at had turned again and was walking parallel to them, glancing now and again keenly in their direction. He was watching Gordon furtively; not a motion escaped him.

There was a moment's delay at the checking counter while the attendant searched for the suitcase, and Gordon was convinced that the man had stopped a few steps away merely for the purpose of watching him.

He dared not look around or notice the man, but he was sure he followed them back to the train. He felt his presence as clearly as if he had been able to see through the back of his head.

But Gordon was cool and collected now. It was as if the experiences of the last two hours, with their embarrassing predicaments, had been wiped off the calendar, and he were back at the moment when he left the Holman house. He knew as well as if he had watched them follow him that they had discovered his — theft — treachery — whatever it ought to be called — and he was being searched for; and because of what was at stake those men would track him to death if they could. But he knew also that his disguise and his companion were for the moment puzzling this sleuth-hound.

This was probably not the only watcher about the station. There were detectives, too, perhaps, hired hastily, and all too ready to seize a suspect.

He marvelled that he could walk so deliberately, swinging his suit-case in his gloved hand at so momentous a time. He smiled and talked easily with the pleasant fellow who walked by his side, and answered his questions with very little idea of what he was saying; making promises which his heart would like to keep, but which he now saw no way of making good.

Thus they entered the train and came to the car where the bride and her mother waited. There were tears on the face of the girl, and she turned to the window to hide them. Gordon's eyes followed her wistfully, and down through the double glass, unnoticed by her absent gaze, he saw the face of the man who had followed them, sharply watching him.

Realizing that his hat was a partial disguise, he kept it on in spite of the presence of the ladies. The color rose in his cheeks that he had to seem so discourteous, but, to cover his embarrassment, he insisted that he be allowed to take the elder lady to the platform, as it really was almost time for the train to start, and so he went deliberately out to act the part of the bridegroom in the face of his recognized foe.

The mother and Gordon stood for a moment on the vestibule platform, while Jefferson bade his sister good-by and tried to soothe her distress at parting from her mother.

"He's all right, Celie, indeed he is," said the young fellow caressingly, laying his hand upon his sister's bowed head. "He's going to be awfully good to you; he cares a lot for you, and he's promised to do all sorts of nice things. He says he'll bring you back soon, and he would never stand in the way of your being with us a lot. He did indeed! What do you think of that? Isn't it quite different from what you thought he would say? He doesn't seem to think he's got to spend the

est of his days in Chicago either. He says there might something turn up that would make it possible for him to change
all his plans. Isn't that great?"

Celia tried to look up and smile through her tears, while
the man outside studied the situation a moment in perplex-
ty and then strolled back to watch Gordon and the elder
woman.

"You will be good to my little girl," he heard the woman's
voice pleading. "She has always been guarded, and she will
miss us all, even though she has you." The voice went
through Gordon like a knife. To stand much more of this and
not denounce himself for a blackguard would be impossible. Neither could he keep his hat on in the presence of this
wonderful motherhood, a motherhood that appealed to him
all the more that he had never known a mother of his own,
and had always longed for one.

He put up his hand and lifted his hat slightly, guarding as
much as possible his own face from the view of the man on
the station platform, who was still walking deliberately, con-
siderately, up and down, often passing near enough to hear
what they were saying. In this reverent attitude, Gordon said,
as though he were uttering a sacred vow:

"I will guard her as if she were — as if I were — as if I
were — *you*" — then he paused a moment and added solemnly,
tenderly — "Mother!"

He wondered if it were not desecration to utter such words
when all the time he was utterly unable to perform them in
the way in which the mother meant. "Impostor!" was the
word which rang in his ears now. The clamor about being
hindered had ceased, for he was doing his best, and not letting even a woman's happiness stand in the way of his duty.

Yet his heart had dictated the words he had spoken, while
his mind and judgment were busy with his perilous position. He could not gainsay his heart, for he felt that in every
way he could he would guard and care for the girl who was
to be in his keeping at least for a few minutes until he could

contrive some way to get her back to her friends without him.

The whistle of the train was sounding now, and the brakemen were shouting, "All aboard!"

He helped the frail little elderly woman down the steps, and she reached up her face to kiss him. He bent and took the caress, the first time that a woman's lips had touched his face since he was a little child.

"Mother, I will not let anything harm her," he whispered, and she said:

"My boy, I can trust you!"

Then he put her into the care of her strong young son, swung upon the train as the wheels began to move, and hurried back to the bride. On the platform, walking beside the train, he still saw the man. Going to the weeping girl, Gordon, stooped over her gently, touched her on the shoulder, and drew the window shade down. The last face he saw outside was the face of the baffled man, who was turning back, but what for? Was he going to report to others, and would there perhaps be another stop before they left the city, where officers or detectives might board the train? He ought to be ready to get off and run for his life if there was. There seemed no way but to fee the porter to look after his companion, and leave her, despicable as it seemed! Yet his soul of honor told him he could never do that, no matter what was at stake.

Then, without warning a new situation was thrust upon him. The bride, who had been standing with bowed head and with her handkerchief up to her eyes, just as her brother had left her, tottered and fell into his arms, limp and white. Instantly all his senses were called into action, and he forgot the man on the platform, forgot the possible next stop in the city, and the explanation he had been about to make to the girl; forgot even the importance of his mission, and the fact that the train he was on was headed toward Chicago, instead of Washington; forgot everything but the fact that the loveliest girl he had ever seen, with the saddest look a human face might wear, was lying apparently lifeless in his arms.

Outside the window the man had turned back and was now running excitedly along with the train trying to see into the window; and down the platform, not ten yards behind, came a frantic man with English-looking clothes, a heavy mustache and goatee, shaggy eyebrows, and a sensual face, striding angrily along as fast as his heavy body would carry him.

But Gordon saw none of them.

6

FIVE hours before, the man who was hurling himself furiously after the rapidly retreating train had driven calmly through the city, from the pier of the White Star Line to the apartment of a man whom he had met abroad, and who had offered him the use of it during his absence. The rooms were in the fourth story of a fine apartment house. The returning exile noted with satisfaction the irreproachable neighborhood, as he slowly descended from the carriage, paid his fee and entered the door, to present his letter of introduction to the janitor in charge.

His first act was to open the steamer trunk which he had brought with him in the cab, and take therefrom his wedding garments. These he carefully arranged on folding hangers and hung in the closet, which was otherwise empty, save for a few boxes piled on the high shelf.

Then he hastened to the telephone and communicated with his best man, Jefferson Hathaway; told him the boat was late arriving at the dock, but that he was here at last; gave him a few directions concerning errands he would like to have done, and agreed to be at the church a half-hour earlier than the time set for the ceremony, to be shown just what arrangements had been made. He was told his bride was feeling very tired and was resting, and agreed that it would be as well not to disturb her; they would have time enough to talk afterward; there really wasn't anything to say but what he had already written. And he would have about all he could do to get there on time as it was. He asked if Jefferson had called for the ring he had ordered and if the carriage would be sent for him in time and then without formalities closed the interview. He and Jefferson were not exactly fond of one another, though Jefferson was the beloved brother of his bride-to-be.

He hung up the receiver and rang for a brandy and soda to brace himself for the coming ordeal which was to bind him to a woman whom for years he had been trying to get in his power and whom he might have loved if she had not dared to scorn him for the evil that she knew was in him. At last he had found a way to subdue her and bring her with her ample fortune to his feet and he felt the exultation of the conqueror as he went about his preparations for the evening.

He made a smug and leisurely toilet, with a smile of satisfaction upon his flabby face. He was naturally a selfish person and had always known how to make other people attend to all bothersome details for him while he enjoyed himself. He was quite comfortable and self-complacent as he posed a moment before the mirror to smooth his mustache and note how well he was looking. Then he went to the closet for his coat.

It was most peculiar, the way it happened, but somehow, as he stepped into that closet to take down his coat, which hung at the back where the space was widest, the opening at the wrist of his shirt-sleeve caught for just an instant in the little knob of the closet latch. The gold button which held the cuff to the wristband slipped its hold, and the man was free almost at once, but the angry twitch he had made at the slight detention had given the door an impetus which set it silently moving on its hinges. (It was characteristic of George

Hayne that he was always impatient of the slightest detention.) He had scarcely put his hand upon his wedding coat
when a soft steel click, followed by utter darkness, warned
him that his impatience had entrapped him. He put out his
hand and pushed at the door, but the catch had settled into
place. It was a very strong, neat little catch, and it did its work
well. The man was a prisoner.

At first he was only annoyed, and gave the door an angry
kick or two, as if of course it would presently release him
meekly; but then he bethought him of his polished wedding
shoes, and desisted. He tried to find a knob and shake the
door, but the only knob was the tiny brass one on the outside of the catch, and you cannot shake a plain surface reared
up before you. Then he set his massive, flabby shoulder
against the door and pressed with all his might, till his bulky
linen shirt front creaked with dismay, and his wedding collar wilted limply. But the door stood like adamant. It was
massive, like the man, but it was not flabby. The wood of
which it was composed had spent its early life in the open
air, drinking only the wine of sunshine and sparkling air, wet
with the dews of heaven, and exercising against the north
blast. It was nothing for it to hold out against this pillow of
a man, who had been nurtured in the dissipation and folly
of a great city. The door held its own, and if doors do such
things, the face of it must have laughed to the silent room;
and who knows but the room winked back? It would be but
natural that a room should resent a new occupant in the absence of a beloved owner.

He was there, safe and fast, in the still dark, with plenty
of time for reflection. And there were things in his life that
called for his reflection. They had never had him at an advantage before.

In due course of time, having exhausted his breath and
strength in fruitless pushing, and his vocabulary in foolish
curses, he lifted up his voice and roared. No other word

would quite describe the sound that issued from his mighty throat. But the city roared placidly below him, and no one minded him in the least.

He sacrificed the shiny toes of the shoes and added resounding kicks on the door to the general hubbub. He changed the roar to a bellow like a mad bull, but still the silence that succeeded it was as deep and monotonous as ever. He tried going to the back of the closet and hurling himself against the door, but he only hurt his soft muscles with the effort. Finally he sat down on the floor of the closet.

Now the janitor's wife, who occupied an apartment somewhat overcrowded, had surreptitiously borrowed the use of this closet the week before, in order to hang therein her Sunday gown, whose front breadth was covered with grease-spots, thickly overlaid with French chalk. The French chalk had done its work and removed the grease-spots, and now lay thickly on the floor of the closet, but the imprisoned bridegroom did not know that, and he sat down quite naturally to rest from his unusual exertions, and to reflect on what could be done next.

The immediate present passed rapidly in review. He could not afford more than ten minutes to get out of this hole. He ought to be on the way to the church at once. There was no knowing what nonsense Celia might get into her head if he delayed. He had known her since her childhood, and she had always scorned him. The hold he had upon her now was like a rope of sand, but only he knew that. If he could but knock that old door down! If he only hadn't hung up his coat in the closet! If the man who built the house only hadn't put such a fool catch on the door! When he got out he would take time to chop it off! If only he had a little more room, and a little more air! It was stifling! Great beads of perspiration went rolling down his hot forehead, and his wet collar made a cool band about his neck. He wondered if he had another clean collar of that particular style with him. If he *only* could get out of this accursed place! Where were all the people? Why was everything so still? Would they never come and let him out?

He reflected that he had told the janitor he would occupy the room with his baggage for two or three weeks perhaps, but he expected to go away on a trip this very evening. The janitor would not think it strange if he did not appear. How would it be to stay here and die? Horrible thought!

He jumped up from the floor and began his howlings and gyrations once more, but soon desisted, and sat down to be entertained by a panorama of his past life which is always unpleasantly in evidence at such times. Fine and clear in the darkness of the closet stood out the nicely laid scheme of deviltry by which he had contrived to be at last within reach of a coveted fortune.

Occasionally would come the frantic thought that just through this little mishap of a foolish clothespress catch he might even yet lose it. The fraud and trickery by which he had an heiress in his power did not trouble him so much as the thought of losing her—at least of losing the fortune. He must have that fortune, for he was deep in debt, and—but then he would refuse to think, and get up to batter at his prison door again.

Four hours his prison walls enclosed him, with inky blackness all around save for a faint glimmer of light, which marked the well-fitted base of the door as the night outside drew on. He had lighted the gas when he began dressing, for the room had already been filled with shadows, and now, it began to seem as if that streak of flickering gas light was the only thing that saved him from losing his mind.

Somewhere from out of the dim shadows a face evolved itself and gazed at him, a haggard face with piercing hollow eyes and despair written upon it. It reproached him with a sin he thought long-forgotten. He shrank back in horror and the cold perspiration stood out upon his forehead, for the eyes were the eyes of the man whose name he had forged upon a note involving trust money fifteen years before; and the man, a quiet, kindly, unsuspecting creature had suffered the penalty in a prison cell until his death some five years ago.

Sometimes at night in the first years after his crime, that face had haunted him, appearing at odd intervals when he was plotting some particularly shady means of adding to his income, until he had resolved to turn over a new leaf, and actually gave up one or two schemes as being too unscrupulous to be indulged in, thus acquiring a comforting feeling of being virtuous. But it was long since the face had come. He had settled it in his mind that the forgery was merely a patch of wild oats which he had sown in his youth, something to be regretted but not too severely blamed for, and thus forgiving himself he had grown to feel that it was more the world's fault for not giving him what he wanted than his own for putting a harmless old man in prison. Of the shame that had killed the old man he knew nothing, nor could have understood. The actual punishment itself was all that appealed to him. He was ever one that had to be taught with the lash, and then only kept straight while it was in sight.

But the face was very near and vivid here in the thick darkness. It was like a cell, this closet, bare, cold, black. The eyes in the gloom seemed to pierce him with the thought: "This is what you made me suffer. It is your turn now. IT IS YOUR TURN NOW!" Nearer and nearer they came looking into his own, until they saw down into his very soul, his little sinful soul, and drew back appalled at the littleness and meanness of what they saw.

Then for the first time in his whole selfish life George Hayne knew any shame, for the eyes read forth to him all that they had seen, and how it looked to them; and beside the tale they told the eyes were clean of sin and almost glad in spite of suffering wrongfully.

Closer and thicker grew the air of the small closet; fiercer grew the rage and shame and horror of the man incarcerated.

Now, from out the shadows there looked other eyes, eyes that had never haunted him before, eyes of victims to whom he had never cast a half a thought. Eyes of men and women he had robbed by his artful, gentlemanly craft; eyes of innocent girls whose wrecked lives had contributed to his selfish scheme of living; even the great reproachful eyes of little children who had looked to him for pity and found none. Last, above them all were the eyes of the lovely girl he was to have married.

He had always loved Celia Hathaway more than he could have loved anyone or anything else besides himself, and it had eaten into his very being that he never could make her bow to him; not even by torture could he bring her to her knees. Stung by the years of her scorn he had stooped lower and lower in his methods of dealing with her until he had come at last to employ the tools of slow torture to her soul that he might bring low her pride and put her fortune and her scornful self within his power. The strength with which she had withheld him until the time of her surrender had turned his selfish love into a hate with contemplations of revenge.

But now her eyes glowed scornfully, wreathed round with bridal white, and seemed to taunt him with his foolish defeat at this last minute before the final triumph.

Undoubtedly the brandy he had taken had gone to his head. Was he going mad that he could not get away from all these terrible eyes?

He felt sure he was dying when at last the janitor came up to the fourth floor on his round of inspection, noticed the light flaring from the transom over the door occupied by the stranger who had said he was going to leave on a trip almost immediately, and went in to investigate. The eyes vanished at his step. The man in the closet lost no time in making his presence known, and the janitor, cautiously, and with great deliberation made careful investigation of the cause and reason for this disturbance and finally let him out, after having received promise of reward which never materialized.

The stranger flew to the telephone in frantic haste, called up the house of his affianced bride, shouting wildly at the operator for all undue delays, and when finally he succeeded in getting some one to the 'phone it was only to be told that neither Mrs. Hathaway nor her son were there. Were they at the church? "Oh, no," the servant answered, "they came back from the church long ago. There is a wedding in the house, and a great many people. They are making so much noise I can't hear. Speak louder, please!"

He shouted and raved at the servant, asking futile questions and demanding information, but the louder he raved the less the servant understood and finally he hung up the receiver and dashed about the room like an insane creature, tearing off his wilted collar, grabbing at another, jerking on his fine coat, searching vainly for his cuffs, snatching his hat and overcoat, and making off down the stairs; breathlessly, regardless of the demand of the janitor for the fee of freedom he had been promised.

Out in the street he rushed hither and thither blindly in search of some conveyance, found a taxicab at last, and, plunging in, ordered it to go at once to the Hathaway address.

Arrived there, he presented an enlivening spectacle to the guests, who were still making merry. His trousers were covered with French chalk, his collar had slipped from its confining button in front and curved gracefully about one fat cheek, his high hat was a crush indeed, having been rammed down to his head in his excitement. He talked so fast and so loud that they thought he was crazy and tried to put him out, but he shook his fist angrily in the face of the footman and demanded to know where Miss Hathaway was. When they told him she was married and gone, he turned livid with wrath and told them that that was impossible, as he was the bridegroom.

By this time the guests had gathered in curious groups in the hall and on the stairs, listening, and when he claimed to be the bridegroom they shouted with laughter, thinking this must be some practical joke or else that the man was insane. But one older gentleman, a friend of the family, stepped up to the excited visitor and said in a quieting voice:

"My friend, you have made a mistake! Miss Hathaway has this evening been married to Mr. George Hayne, just arrived from abroad, and they are at this moment on their way to take the train. You have come too late to see her, or else you have the wrong address, and are speaking of some other Miss Hathaway. That is very likely the explanation."

George looked around on the company with helpless rage, then rushed to his taxicab and gave the order for the station.

Arriving at the station, he saw it was within half a minute of departure of the Chicago train, and none knew better than he what time that train had been going to depart. Had he not given minute directions regarding the arrangements to his future brother-in-law? What did it all mean anyway? Had Celia managed somehow to carry out the wedding without him to hide her mortification at his non-appearance? Or had she run away? He was too excited to use his reason. He could merely urge his heavy bulk onward toward the fast fleeing train; and dashed up the platform, overcoat streaming from his arm, coat-tails flying, hat crushed down upon his head, his fat, bechalked legs rumbling heavily after him. He passed Jefferson and his mother; watching tearfully, lingeringly, the retreating mother did not notice and only said absently; "I think he'll be good to her, don't you, Jeff? He has nice eyes. I don't remember that his eyes used to seem so pleasant, and so — deferential." Then they turned to go back to their car, and the train moved faster and faster out of the station. It would presently rush away out into the night, leaving the two pursuers to face each other, baffled.

Both realized this at the same instant and the short, thick-set man with sudden decision turned again and plunging along with the train caught at the rail and swung himself with dangerous precipitation to the last platform of the last car with a half-frightened triumph. Looking back he saw the other man with a frantic effort sprint forward, trying to do the same thing, and failing in the attempt, sprawl flat on the platform, to the intense amusement of a couple of trainmen standing near.

George Hayne, having thus come to a full stop in his headlong career, lay prostrate for a moment, stunned and shaken; then gathered himself up slowly and stood gazing after the departing train. After all, if he caught it what could he have done? It was incredible that Celia could have got herself married and gone on her wedding trip without him. If she had eloped with some one else and they were on that train what could he have done? Kill the bridegroom and force the bride to return with him and be married over again? Yes, but that might have been a trifle awkward after all, and he had enough awkward situations to his account already. Besides, it wasn't in the least likely that Celia was married yet. Those people at the house had been fooled somehow, and she had run away. Perhaps her mother and brother were gone with her. The same threats that had made her bend to him once should follow her wherever she had gone. She would marry him yet and pay for this folly a hundred fold. He lifted a shaking hand of execration toward the train which by this time was vanishing into the dark opening at the end of the station, where signal lights like red berries festooned themselves in an arch against the blackness, and the lights of the last car paled and vanished like a forgotten dream.

Then he turned and hobbled slowly back to the gates regardless of the merriment he was arousing in the genial trainmen; for he was spent and bruised, and his appearance was anything but dignified. No member of the wedding company had they seen him at this juncture would have recognized in him any resemblance to the handsome gentleman who had played his part in the wedding ceremony. No one would have thought it possible that he could be Celia Hathaway's bridegroom.

Slowly back to the gate he crept, haggard, dishevelled, crestfallen; his hair in its several isolate locks downfallen over his forehead, his collar wilted, his clothes smeared with chalk and dust, his overcoat dragging forlornly behind him. He was trying to decide what to do next, and realizing the torment of a perpetual thirst, when a hand was laid suddenly upon him and a voice that somehow had a familiar twang, said: "You will come with me, sir."

He looked up and there before him in the flesh were the eyes of the man who had haunted him for years, the eyes grown younger, and filled with more than reproach. They were piercing him with the keenness of retribution. They said, as plainly as those eyes in the closet had spoken but a brief hour before: "Your time is over. My time has come. You have sinned. You shall suffer. Come now and meet your reward."

He started back in horror. His hands trembled and his brain reeled. He wished for another cocktail to help him to meet this most extraordinary emergency. Surely, something had happened to his nerves that he was seeing these eyes in reality and hearing the voice, that old man's voice made young, bidding him come with him. It could not be, of course. He was unnerved with all he had been through. The man had mistaken him for some one—or perhaps it was not a man after all. He glanced quickly around to see if others saw him, and at once became aware that a crowd was collecting about them.

The man with the strange eyes and the familiar voice was dressed in plain clothes, but he seemed to have full assurance that he was a real live man and had a right to dictate. George Hayne could not shake away his grasp. There was a determination about it that struck terror to his soul, and he had a weak desire to scream and hide his eyes. Could he be coming down with delirium tremens? That brandy must have been unusually strong to have lasted so long in its effects. Then he made a weak effort to speak, but his voice sounded small and frightened. The eyes took his assurance from him.

"Who are you?" he asked, and meant to add, "What right have you to dictate to *me?*" but the words died away in his throat, for the plainclothes man had opened his coat and disclosed a badge that shone with a sinister light straight into his eyes.

"I am Norman Brand," answered the voice, "and I want you for what you did to my father. It is time you paid your debt. You were the cause of his humiliation and death. I have been watching you for years. I saw the notice of your wedding in the paper and was tracking you. It was for this I entered the service. Come with me."

With a cry of horror George Hayne wrenched away from his captor and turned to flee, but instantly three revolvers were levelled at him, and he found that two policemen in brass buttons were stationed behind him, and the crowd closed in about him. Wherever he turned it was to look into the barrel of a gun, and there was no escape in any direction.

They led him away to the patrol wagon, the erstwhile bridegroom, and in place of the immaculate linen he had searched so frantically for in his apartment they put upon his wrists cuffs of iron. They put him in a cell and left him with the eyes of the old man for company and the haunting likeness of his son's voice filling him with frenzy.

The unquenchable thirst came upon him and he begged for brandy and soda, but none came to slake his thirst, for he had crossed the great gulf and justice at last had him in her grasp.

7

MEANWHILE the man on the steps of the last car of the Chicago Limited was having his doubts about whether he ought to have boarded that train. He realized that the fat traveller who was hurling himself after the train had stirred in him a sudden impulse which had been only half formed before and he had obeyed it. Perhaps he was following a wrong scent and would lose the reward which he knew was his if he brought the thief of the code-writing, dead or alive, to his employer. He was half inclined to jump off again now before it was too late; but looking down he saw they were already speeding over a network of tracks, and trains were flying by in every direction. By the time they were out of this the speed would be too great for him to attempt a jump. It was even now risky, and he was heavy for athletics. He must do it at once if he did it at all.

He looked ahead tentatively to see if the track on which he must jump was clear, and the great eye of an engine stabbed him in the face, as it bore down upon him. The next instant it swept by, its hot breath fanning his cheek, and he drew back shuddering involuntarily. It was of no use. He could not jump here. Perhaps they would slow up or stop, and anyway, should he jump or stay on board?

He sat down on the upper step the better to get the situation in hand. Perhaps in a minute more the way would be clearer to jump off if he decided not to go on. Thus he vacillated. It was rather unlike him not to know his own mind.

It seemed as if there must be something here to follow, and yet, perhaps he was mistaken. He had been the first man of the company at the front door after Mr. Holman turned the paper over, and they all had noticed the absence of the red mark. It had been simultaneous with the clicking of the door-latch and he had covered the ground from his seat to the door sooner than anyone else. He could swear he had seen the man get into the cab that stood almost in front of the house. He had lost no time in getting into his own car which was detailed for such an emergency, and in signalling the officer on a motor-cycle who was also ready for a quick call. The carriage had barely turned the corner when they followed, there was no other of the kind in sight either way but that, and he had followed it closely. It must have been the right carriage. And yet, when the man got out at the church he was changed, much changed in appearance, so that he had looked twice into the empty carriage to make sure that the man for whom he searched was not still in there hiding. Then he had followed him into the church and seen him married; stood close at hand when he put his bride into a big car, and he had followed the car to the house where the reception was held; even mingling with the guests and watching until the bridal couple left for the train. He had stood in the alley in the shadow, the only one of the guests who had found how the bride was really going away, and again he had followed to the station.

He had walked close enough to the bridegroom in the station to be almost sure that mustache and those heavy eyebrows were false; and yet he could not make it out. How could it be possible that a man who was going to be married in a great church full of fashionable people would dare to flirt with chance as to accept an invitation to a dinner where he might not be able to get away for hours? What would have happened if he had not got there in time? Was it in the least possible that these two men could be identical? Everything but the likeness and the fact that he had followed the man so closely pointed out the impossibility.

The thick-set man was accustomed to trust his inner impressions thoroughly, and in this case his inner impression was that he must watch this peculiar bridegroom and be sure he was not the right man before he forever got away from him — and yet — and yet, he might be missing the right man by doing it. However, he had come so far, he risked a good deal already in following and in throwing himself on that fast moving train. He would stay a little longer and find out for sure. He would try and get a seat where he could watch him and in an hour he ought to be able to tell if he were really the man who had stolen the code-writing. If he could avoid the conductor for a time he would simply profess to have taken the wrong train by mistake, and maybe could get put off somewhere near home, in case he discovered that he was barking up the wrong tree. He would stick to the train for a little yet, inasmuch as there seemed no safe way of getting off at present.

Having decided so much, he gave one last glance toward the twinkling lights of the city hurrying past, and getting up sauntered into the train, keeping a weather eye out for the conductor. He meant to burn no bridges behind him. He was well provided with money for any kind of a tip and mileage books and passes. He knew where to send a telegram that would bring him instant assistance in case of need, and even now he knew the officer on the motor-cycle had reported to his employer that he had boarded this train. There was really no immediate need for him to worry. It was big game he was after and one must take some risks in a case of that sort. Thus he entered the sleeper to make good the impression of his inner senses.

Gordon had never held anything so precious, so sweet and beautiful and frail-looking, in his arms. He had a feeling that he ought to lay her down, yet there was a longing to draw her closer to himself and shield her from everything that could trouble her.

But she was not his—only a precious trust to be guarded and cared for as vigilantly as the message he carried hidden about his neck; she belonged to another, somewhere, and was a sacred trust until circumstances made it possible for him to return her to her rightful husband. Just what all this might mean to himself, to the woman in his arms, and to the man who she was to have married, Gordon had not as yet had time to think. It was as if he had been watching a moving picture and suddenly a lot of circumstances had fallen in a heap and become all jumbled up together, the result of his own rash but unsuspecting steps, the way whole families have in moving pictures of falling through a sky-scraper from floor to floor, carrying furniture and inhabitants with them as they descend.

He had not as yet been able to disentangle himself from the debris and find out what had been his fault and what he ought to do about it.

He laid her gently on the couch of the drawing-room and opened the little door of the private dressing-room. There would be cold water in there.

He knew very little about caring for sick people—he had always been well and strong himself—but cold water was what they used for people who had fainted, he was sure. He would not call in anyone to help, unless it was absolutely necessary. He pulled the door of the stateroom shut, and went after the water. As he passed the mirror, he started at the curious vision of himself. One false eyebrow had come loose and was hanging over his eye, and his goatee was crooked. Had it been so all the time? He snatched the eyebrow off, and then the other; but the mustache and goatee were more tightly affixed, and it was very painful to remove them. He glanced back, and the white limp look of the girl on the couch frightened him. What was he about, to stop over his appearance when she might be dying, and as for pain—he tore the false hair roughly from him, and stuffing it into his pocket, filled a glass with water and went back to the couch. His chin and upper lip smarted, but he did not tice it, nor know that the mark of the plaster was all about his face. He only knew that she lay there apparently lifeless before him, and he must bring the soul back into those dear eyes. It was strange, wonderful, how his feeling had grown for the girl whom he had never seen till three hours before.

He held the glass to her white lips and tried to make her drink, then poured water on his handkerchief and awkwardly bathed her forehead. Some hairpins slipped loose and a great wealth of golden-brown hair fell across his knees as he half knelt beside her. One little hand drooped over the side of the couch and touched his. He started! It seemed so soft and cold and lifeless.

He blamed himself that he had no remedies in his suitcase. Why had he never thought to carry something,—a simple restorative? Other people might need it though he did not. No man ought to travel without something for the saving of life in an emergency. He might have needed it himself even, in case of a railroad accident or something.

He slipped his arm tenderly under her head and tried to raise it so that she could drink, but the white lips did not move nor attempt to swallow.

Then a panic seized him. Suppose she was dying? Not until later, when he had quiet and opportunity for thought, did it occur to him what a terrible responsibility he had dared to take upon himself in letting her people leave her with him; what a fearful position he would have been in if she had really died. At the moment his whole thought was one of anguish at the idea of losing her; anxiety to save her precious life; and not for himself.

Forgetting his own need of quiet and obscurity, he laid her gently back upon the couch again, and rushed from the stateroom out into the aisle of the sleeper. The conductor was just making his rounds and he hurried to him with a white face.

"Is there a doctor on board, or have you any restoratives? There is a lady—" He hesitated and the color rolled freshly into his anxious face. "That is—my wife." He spoke the word unwillingly, having at the instant of speaking realized that he must say this to protect her good name. It seemed like uttering a falsehood, or stealing another man's property; and yet, technically, it was true, and for her sake at least he must acknowledge it.

"My wife," he began again more connectedly, "is ill—unconscious."

The conductor looked at him sharply. He had sized them up as a wedding party when they came down the platform toward the train. The young man's blush confirmed his supposition.

"I'll see!" he said briefly. "Go back to her and I'll bring some one."

It was just as Gordon turned back that the thick-set man entered the car from the other end and met him face to face, but Gordon was too distraught at that moment to notice him, for his mind was at rest about his pursuer as soon as the train started.

Not so with the pursuer however. His keen little eyes took in the white, anxious face, the smear of sticking plaster about the mouth and eyebrows, and instantly knew his man. His instincts had not failed him after all.

He put out a pair of brawny fists to catch at him, but a lurch of the train and Gordon's swift stride out-purposed him, and by the time the little man had righted his footing Gordon was disappearing into the stateroom, and the conductor with another man was in the aisle behind him waiting to pass. He stepped back and watched. At least he had driven his prey to quarry and there was no possible escape now until the train stopped. He would watch that door as a cat watches a mouse, and perhaps be able to send a telegram for help before he made any move at all. It was as well that his impulse to take the man then and there had come to naught. What would the other passengers have thought of him? He must of course move cautiously. What a blunder he had almost made. It was not part of his purpose to make public his errand. The men who were behind him did not wish to be known, nor to have their business known.

With narrowing eyes he watched the door of the stateroom as the conductor and doctor came and went. He gathered from a few questions asked by one of the passengers that there was some one sick, probably the lady he had seen faint as the train started. It occurred to him that this might be his opportunity, and when the conductor came out of the drawing-room the second time he inquired if any assistance was needed, and implied that doctoring was his profession, though it would be a sorry patient that had only his attention. However, if he had one accomplishment it was bluffing, and he never stopped at any profession that suited his needs.

The conductor was annoyed at the interruptions that had already occurred and he answered him brusquely that they had all the help necessary and there wasn't anything the matter anyway.

There was nothing left for the man to do but wait.

He subsided with his eye on the stateroom door, and later secured a berth in plain sight of that door, but gave no order to have it made up until every other passenger in the car was gone to what rest a sleeping car provides. He kept his vigil well, but was rewarded with no sight of his prey that night, and at last with a sense of duty well done and the comfortable promise from the conductor that his deftly worded telegraphic message to Mr. Holman should be sent from a station they passed a little after midnight, he crept to his well-earned rest. He was not at home in a dress shirt and collar, being of the walks of life where a collar is mostly accounted superfluous, and he was glad to be relieved of it for a few hours. It had not yet occurred to him that his appearance in that evening suit would be a trifle out of place when morning came. It is doubtful if he had ever considered matters of dress. His profession was that of a human ferret of the lower order, and there were many things he did not know. It might have been the way he held his fork at dinner that had made Gordon decide that he was but a henchman of the others.

Having put his mind and his body at rest he proceeded to sleep, and the train thundered on its way into the night.

Gordon meanwhile had hurried back from his appeal to the conductor, and stood looking helplessly down at the delicate girl as she lay there so white and seemingly lifeless. Her pretty travelling gown set off the exquisite face finely; her glorious hair seemed to crown her. A handsome hat had fallen unheeded to the floor, and lay rolling back and forth in the aisle with the motion of the train. He picked it up reverently, as though it had been a part of her. His face in the few minutes had gone haggard.

The conductor hurried in presently, followed by a grave elderly man with a professional air. He touched a practised finger to the limp wrist, looked closely into the face, and then taking a little bottle from a case he carried called for a glass.

The liquid was poured between the closed lips, the white throat reluctantly swallowed it, the eyelids presently fluttered, a long breath that was scarcely more than a sigh hovered between the lips, and then the blue eyes opened.

She looked about, bewildered, looking longest at Gordon, then closed her eyes wearily, as if she wished they had not brought her back, and lay still.

The physician still knelt beside her, and Gordon, with time now to think, began to reflect on the possible consequences of his deeds. With anxious face, he stood watching, reflecting bitterly that he might not claim even a look of recognition from those sweet eyes, and wishing with all his heart that his marriage had been genuine. A passing memory of his morning ride to New York in company with Miss Bentley's conjured vision brought wonder to his eyes. It all seemed so long ago, and so strange that he ever could have entertained for a moment the thought of marrying Julia. She was a good girl of course, fine and handsome and all that, — but — and here his eyes sought the sweet sad face on the couch, and his heart suffered in a real agony for the trouble he saw; and for the trouble he must yet give her when he told her who he was, or rather who he was not; for he must tell her and that soon. It would not do to go on in her company — nor to Chicago! And yet, how was he possibly to leave her in this condition?

But no revelations were to be given that night.

The physician administered another draught, and ordered the porter to make up the berth immediately. Then with skillful hands and strong arms he laid the young girl in upon the pillows and made her comfortable, Gordon meanwhile standing awkwardly by with averted eyes and troubled mien. He would have like to help, but he did not know how.

"She'd better not be disturbed any more than is necessary to-night," said the doctor, as he pulled the pretty cloth travelling gown smoothly down about the girl's ankles and patted it with professional hands. "Don't let her yield to any nonsense about putting up her hair, or taking off that frock for fear she'll rumple it. She needs to lie perfectly quiet. It's a case of utter exhaustion, and I should say a long strain of some kind — anxiety, worry perhaps." He looked keenly at the sheepish bridegroom. "Has she had any trouble?"

Gordon lifted honest eyes.

"I'm afraid so," he answered contritely, as if it must have been his fault some way.

"Well, don't let her have any more," said the elder man briskly. "She's a very fragile bit of womanhood, young man, and you'll have to handle her carefully or she'll blow away.

Make her *happy,* young man! People can't have too much happiness in this world. It's the best thing, after all, to keep them well. Don't be afraid to give her plenty."

"Thank you!" said Gordon, fervently, wishing it were in his power to do what the physician ordered.

The kindly physician, the assiduous porter, and the brusque but good-hearted conductor went away at last, and Gordon was left with his precious charge, who to all appearances was sleeping quietly. The light was turned low and the curtains of the berth were a little apart. He could see the dim outline of drapery about her, and one shadowy hand lying limp at the edge of the couch, in weary relaxation.

Above her, in the upper berth, which he had told the porter not to make up, lay the great purple-black plumed hat, and a sheaf of lilies of the valley from her bouquet. It seemed all so strange for him to be there in their sacred presence.

He locked the door, so that no one should disturb the sleeper, and went slowly into the little private dressing-room. For a full minute after he reached it, he stood looking into the mirror before him, looking at his own weary, soiled face, and wondering if he, Cyril Gordon, heretofore honored and self-respecting, had really done in the last twelve hours all the things which he was crediting himself with having done! And the question was, how had it happened? Had he taken leave his senses, or had circumstances been too much for him? Had he lost the power of judging between right and wrong? Could he have helped any of the things that had come upon him? How could he have helped them? What ought he to have done? What ought he to do now? Was he a criminal beyond redemption? Had he spoiled the life of the sweet woman out there in her berth, or could he somehow make amends for what he had done? And was he as badly to blame for it all as he felt himself to be?

After a minute he rallied, to realize that his face was dirty. He washed the marks of the adhesive plaster away, and then, not satisfied with the result, he brought his shaving things from his suit-case and shaved. Somehow, he felt more like himself after his toilet was completed, and he slipped back into the darkened drawing-room and stretched himself wearily on the couch, which, according to his directions, was not made up, but merely furnished with pillows and a blanket.

The night settled into the noisy quiet of an express train, and each revolution of the wheels, as they whirled their way Chicagoward, resolved itself into the old refrain, "Don't let anything hinder you! Don't let anything hinder you!"

He certainly was not taking the most direct route from New York to Washington, though it might eventually prove that the longest way round was the shortest way home, on account of its comparative safety.

As he settled to the quiet of his couch, a number of things came more clearly to his vision. One was that they had safely passed the outskirts of New York without interference of any kind, and must by this time be speeding toward Albany, unless they were on a road that took them more directly West. He had not thought to look at the tickets for knowledge of his bearings, and the light was too dim for him to make out any monograms or letterings on inlaid wood panels or transoms, even if he had known enough about New York railroads to gain information from them. There was one thing certain: even if he had been mistaken about his supposed pursuers, by morning there would surely be some one searching for him. The duped Holman combination would stop at nothing when they discovered his theft of the paper, and he could not hope that so sharp-eyed a man as Mr. Holman had seemed to be would be long in discovering the absence of his private mark on the paper. Undoubtedly he knew it already. As for the frantic bridegroom, Gordon dreaded the thought of meeting him. It must be put off at any hazards until the message was safe with his chief, then, if he had to answer with his life for carrying off another man's bride, he could at least feel that he left no duty to his government undone. It was plain that his present situation was a dangerous one from two points of view, for the bridegroom would have no difficulty in finding out what train he and the lady had taken, and he was satisfied that an emissary of Holman had more than a suspicion of his identity. The obvious thing to do was to get off that train at the first opportunity and get across country to another line of railroad. But how was that to be done with a sick lady on his hands? Of course he could leave her to herself. She probably had taken journeys before, and would know how to get back. She would at least be able to telegraph to her friends to come for her. He could leave her money and a note explaining his involuntary villainy, and her indignation with him would probably be a sufficient stimulant to keep her from dying of chagrin at her plight. But as from the first every nerve and fibre in him rejected this suggestion. It would be cowardly, unmanly, horrible! Undoubtedly it might be the wise thing to do from many standpoints, but — *never!* He could no more leave her that way than he could run off to save his life and leave that message he carried. She was a trust as much as that. He had got into this, and he must get out somehow, but he would not desert the lady or neglect his duty.

Toward morning, when his fitful vigil became less lucid it occurred to him that he ought really to have deserted the bride while she was still unconscious, jumping off the train at the short stop they made soon after she fell into his arms. She would then have been cared for by some one, his absence discovered, and she would have been put off the train and her friends sent for at once. But it would have been dastardly to have deserted her that way not knowing even if she still lived, he on whom she had at least a claim of temporary protection.

It was all a terrible muddle, right and wrong juggled in such a mysterious and unusual way. He never remembered to have come to a spot before where it was difficult to know which of two things it was right to do. There had always before been such clearly defined divisions. He had supposed that people who professed not to know what was right were people who wished to be blinded on the subject because they wished to do wrong and think it right. But now he saw that he had judged such too harshly.

Perhaps his brain had been overstrained with the excitement and annoyances of the day, and he was not quite in a condition to judge what was right. He ought to snatch a few minutes' sleep, and then his mind would be clearer, for something must be done and that soon. It would not do to risk entering a large city where detectives and officers with full particulars might even now be on the watch for him. He was too familiar with the workings of retribution in this progressive age not to know his danger. But he really must get some sleep.

At last he yielded to the drowsiness that was stealing over him—just for a moment, he thought, and the wheels hummed on their monotonous song: "Don't let anything hinder! Don't let anything—! Don't let—! Don't! Hinder-r-r-r!"

8

THE man slept, and the train rushed on. The night waned. The dawn grew purple in the east, and streaked itself with gold; then later got out a fillet of crimson and drew over its cloudy forehead. The breath of the lilies filled the little room with delicate fragrance, and mingled strange scenes in the dreams of the man and the woman so strangely united.

The sad little bride grew restless and stirred, but the man on the couch did not hear her. He was dreaming of a shooting affray, in which he carried a bride in a gold pencil and was shot for stealing a sandwich out of Mr. Holman's vest pocket.

The morning light grew clearer. The east had put on a vesture of gold above her purple robe, and its reflection shone softly in at the window, for the train was just at that moment rushing northward, though its general course was west.

The sleeper behind the thick green curtains stirred again and became conscious, as in many days past, of her heavy burden of sorrow. Always at first waking the realization of it sat upon her as though it would crush the life from her body. Lying still with bated breath, she fought back waking consciousness as she had learned to do in the last three months, yet knew it to be futile while she was doing it.

The sun shot up between the bars of crimson, like a topaz on a lady's gown that crowns the whole beautiful costume. The piercing, jewelled light lay across the white face, touched the lips with warm fingers, and the troubled soul knew all that had passed.

She lay quiet, letting the torrent sweep over her with its sickening realization. She was married! It was over—with the painful parting from dear ones. She was off away from them all. The new life she so dreaded had begun, and how was she to face it—the life with one whom she feared and did not respect? How could she ever have done it but for the love of her dear ones?

Gradually she came to remember the night before—the parting with her mother and her brother; the little things that brought the tears again to her eyes. Then all was blankness. She must have fainted. She did not often faint, but it must be—yes, she remembered opening her eyes and seeing men's faces about her, and George—could it have been George?—with a kinder look in his eyes than she had ever thought to see there. Then she must have fainted again—or had she? No, some one had lifted her into this berth, and she had drunk something and had gone to sleep. What had happened? Where was everybody? It was good to have been left alone. She grudgingly gave her unloved husband a fragment of gratitude for not having tried to talk to her. In the carriage on the way he had seemed determined to begin a long argument of some kind. She did not want to argue any more. She had written tomes upon the subject, and had said all she had to say. He was not deceived. He knew she did not love him, and would never have married him but for her mother's sake and for the sake of her beloved father's memory. What was the use of saying more? Let it rest. The deed was done, and they were married. Now let him have his way and make her suffer as he chose. If he would but let her suffer in silence and not inflict his bitter tongue upon her, she would try to bear it. And perhaps — oh, perhaps, she would not live long, and it would soon be all over.

As the daylight grew, the girl felt an inclination to find out whether her husband was near. Cautiously she lifted her head and, drawing back a corner of the curtain, peered out.

He lay quietly on the couch, one hand under his cheek against the pillow, the other across his breast, as if to guard something. He was in the still sleep of the over-wearied. He scarcely seemed to be breathing.

Celia dropped the curtain, and put her hand to her throat. It startled her to find him so near and so still. Softly, stealthily, she lay down again and closed her eyes. She must not waken him. She would have as long a time to herself as was possible, and try to think of her dear mother and her precious brother. Oh, if she were just going away from them alone, how well she could bear it! But to be going with one whom she had always almost hated—

Her brother's happy words about George suddenly came to her mind. Jefferson had thought him fine. Well, of course the dear boy knew nothing about it. He had not read all those letters — those awful letters. He did not know the threats — the terrible language that had been used. She shuddered as she thought of it. But in the same breath she was glad that her brother had been deceived. She would not have it otherwise. Her dear ones must never know what she had gone through to save them from disgrace and loss of fortune — disgrace, of course, being the first and greatest. She had feared that George would let them see through his veneer of manners, and leave them troubled, but he had made a better appearance than she had hoped. The years had made a greater change in him than she had expected. He really had not been so bad as her conjured image of him.

Then a sudden desire to look at him again seized her, to know once for all just how he really did seem. She would not want to notice him awake any more than she could help, nor dare, lest he presume upon her sudden interest, to act as if he had never offended; but if she should look at him now as he lay asleep she might study his face and see what she really had to expect.

She fought the desire to peer at him again, but finally it gained complete possession of her, and she drew back the curtain once more.

He was lying just as quietly as before. His heavy hair, a little disordered on the pillow, gave him a noble, interesting appearance. He did not seem at all a fellow of whom to be afraid. It was incredible that he could have written those letters.

She tried to trace in his features a likeness to the youth of ten years ago, whom she had known when she was but a little girl, who had tied her braids to her chair, and put raw oysters and caterpillars down her back, or stretched invisible cords to trip her feet in dark places; who made her visits to a beloved uncle—whom he also had the right to call uncle, though he was no cousin of hers—a long list of catastrophes resulting in tears; who had never failed to mortify her on all occasions possible, and once—But the memories were too horrible as they crowded one upon another! Let them be forgotten!

She watched the face before her keenly, critically, yet she could see no trace of any such character as she had imagined the boy George must have developed as a man; of which his letters had given her ample proof. This man's face was finely cut and sensitive. There was nothing coarse or selfish in its lines. The long, dark lashes lay above dark circles of weariness, and gave that look of boyishness that always touches the maternal chord in a woman's heart. George used to have a puffy, self-indulgent look under his eyes even when he was a boy. She had imagined from his last photograph that he would be much stouter, much more bombastic; but, then, in his sleep, perhaps those things fell from a man.

She tried to turn away indifferently, but something in his face held her. She studied it. If he had been any other man, any stranger, she would have said from looking at him critically that kindness and generosity, self-respect and respect for women, were written all over the face before her. There was fine, firm modelling about the lips and the clean-shaven chin; and about the forehead the look almost of a scholar; yet she thought she knew the man before her to be none of these things. How deceptive were looks! She would probably be envied rather than pitied by all who saw her. Well, perhaps that was better. She could the easier keep her trouble to herself. But stay, what was there about this man that seemed different? The smooth face? Yes. She had the dim impression that last night he wore a mustache. She must have been mistaken, of course. She had only looked at him when absolutely necessary, and her brain was in such a whirl; but still there seemed to be something different about him.

Her eyes wandered to the hand that lay across his breast. It was the fine white hand of the professional man, the kind of hand that somehow attracts the eye with a sense of cleanness and strength. There was nothing flabby about it. George as a boy used to have big, stumpy fingers and nails chewed down to the quick. She could remember how she used to hate to look at them when she was a little girl, and yet somehow could not keep her eyes away. She saw with relief that the nails on his hand were well shaped and well cared for.

He looked very handsome and attractive as he lay there. The sun shot one of its early daring bolts of light across his hair as the train turned in its course and lurched northward around a curve. It glinted there for a moment, like a miniature searchlight, travelling over the head, showing up every wave and curve. He had the kind of hair which makes a woman's hand instinctively long to touch it.

Celia wondered at the curious thoughts that crowded through her mind, knowing that all the while there was the consciousness that when this man should wake she would think of nothing but his hateful personality as she had known it through the years. And she was his wife! How strange! How terrible! How impossible to live with the thought through interminable weary years! Oh, that she might die at once before her strength failed and her mother found out her sorrow!

She lay back again on her pillows very still and tried to think, but somehow a pleasant image of him, her husband, lingered in her memory. Could it be possible that she would ever see anything pleasant in him? Ever endure the days of his companionship? Ever come to the point where she could overlook his outrageous conduct toward her, forgive him, and be even tolerant of him? Sharp memories crowded upon her, and the smarting years stung their way into her eyes, answering and echoing in her heart, "No, no, a thousand times, no!" She had paid his price and gained redemption for her own, but—forget what he had done? *Never!*

The long strain of weariness, and the monotony of the onrushing train, lulled her into unconsciousness again, and the man on the couch slumbered on.

He came to himself suddenly, with all his senses on the alert, as the thumping noise and the motion of the train ceased, and a sudden silence of open country succeeded, broken now and again by distant oncoming and receding voices. He caught the fragment of a sentence from some train official: "It's a half-hour late, and maybe more. We'll just have to lie by, that's all. Here, you, Jim, take this flag and run up to the switch—" The voice trailed into the distance, ended by the metallic note of a hammer doing something mysterious to the under-pinning of the car.

Gordon sat up suddenly, his hand yet across his breast where his first waking thought had been to feel if the little pencil-case were safe.

Glancing stealthily toward the curtains of the berth, and perceiving no motion, he concluded that the girl still slept.

Softly he slipped his feet into his shoes, gave one or two other touches to his toilet, and stood up, looking toward the curtains. He wanted to go out and see where they were stopping, but dared he go without knowing that she was all right?

Softly, reverently, he stooped and brought his face close to the opening in the curtains. Celia felt his eyes upon her. Her own were closed, and by a superhuman effort she controlled her breathing, slowly, gently, as if she were asleep.

He looked for a long moment, thrilled by the delicate beauty of her sleeping face, filled with an intoxicating joy to see that her lips were no longer white; then, turning reverently away, he unlocked the door and stepped forth.

The other occupants of the car were still wrapped in slumber. Loud snores of various kinds and qualities testified to that. A dim light at the further end contended luridly, and losingly, with the daylight now flooding the outside world and creeping mischievously into the transoms.

Gordon closed the door of the compartment noiselessly and went down the aisle to the end of the car.

A door was open, and he could hear voices outside. The conductor stood talking with two brakemen. He heard the words: "Three-quarters of an hour at least," and then the men walked off toward the engine.

Gordon looked across the country, and for the first time since he started on his journey let himself remember that it was springtime and May.

There had been a bitter wind the night before, with a hint of rain in the air. In fact, it had rained quite smartly during the ride to the hospital with that hurt child, but he had been so perturbed that he had taken little notice of the weather. But this was a radiant morning.

The sun was in one of its most charming moods, when it touches everything with a sort of unnatural glory after the long winter of darkness and cold. Every tree trunk in the distance seemed to stand out clearly, every little grass-blade was set with a glowing jewel, and the winding stream across a narrow valley fairly blazed with brightness. The very road with its deep, clean wheel-groves seemed like a well-taken photograph.

The air had an alluring softness mingled with its tang of winter that made one long to take a walk anywhere out into the world, just for the joy of being and doing. A meadow-lark shot up from somewhere to a telegraph pole, let go a blithe note, and hurried on. It was glorious. The exhilaration filled Gordon's blood.

And here was the chance he craved to slip away from the train before it reached a place where he could be discovered. If he had but thought to bring his suit-case! He could slip back now without being noticed and get it! He could even go without it! But—he could not leave her that way—could he? Ought he? Perhaps he ought—But it would not do to leave his suit-case with her, for it contained letters addressed to his real name. An explanation would of course be demanded, and he could never satisfy a loving mother and brother for having left a helpless girl in such a situation—even if he could satisfy his own conscience, which he knew he never could. He simply could not leave her, and yet he *must* get away from that train as soon as possible. Perhaps this was the only opportunity he would have before reaching Buffalo, and it was very risky, indeed dangerous, to dare enter Buffalo. It was a foregone conclusion that there would be private detectives ready to meet the train in Buffalo with full descriptions and particulars and only too ready to make way with him if they could do so without being found out. He looked nervously back at the door of the car. Dared he attempt to waken her and say that they had made a mistake and must change cars? Was she well enough? And where could they go?

He looked off toward the landscape for answer to his question.

They were decidedly in the country. The train stood at the top of a high embankment of cinders, below which was a smooth country road running parallel to the railroad for some distance till it met another road at right angles to it, which stretched away between thrifty meadow-lands to a nestling village. The glorified stream he had first noticed far up the valley glinted narrower here in the morning light, with a suggestion of watercress and forget-me-nots in its fringes as it veered away under a bridge toward the village and hid itself in a tangle of willows and cat-tails.

How easy it would be to slide down that embankment, and walk out that road over the bridge to the village, where of course a conveyance of some sort could be hired to bear him to another railroad town and thence to — Pittsburgh, perhaps, where he could easily get a train to Washington. How easy if only he were not held by some invisible hands to care for the sweet sleeper inside the car! And yet, for her sake as well as his own, he must do something, and that right speedily.

He was standing thus in deep meditation, looking off at the little village which seemed so near and yet would be so far for her to walk, when he was pervaded with that strange sense of some one near. For an instant he resisted the desire to lift his eyes and prove to himself that no one was present in a doorway which a moment before he knew had been unoccupied. Then, frowning at his own nervousness, he turned.

She stood there in all the beauty of her fresh young girlhood, a delicate pallor on her cheeks, and a deep sadness in her great dark eyes, which were fixed upon him intently, in a sort of puzzled study. She was fully dressed, even to her hat and gloves. Every wave of her golden hair lay exquisitely in place under the purple hat, as though she might have taken an hour or two at her toilet; yet she had made it with excited haste, and with trembling fingers, determined to have it accomplished before the return of her dreaded liege lord.

She had sprung from her berth the instant he closed the door upon her, and fastened the little catch to bar him out. She had dashed cold water into her face, fastened her garments hurriedly, and tossed the glory of her hair into place with a few touches and what hairpins she could find on the floor. Then putting on her hat, coat, and gloves, she had followed him into the outer air. She had a feeling that she must have air to breathe or she would suffocate. A wild desire filled her to go alone into the great out-of-doors. Oh, if she but dared to run away from him! But that she might not do, for all his threats would then probably be made good by him upon her dear mother and brother. No, she must be patient and bear to the end all that was set down for her. But she would get out and breathe a little before he returned. He had very likely gone into the smoker. She remembered that the George of old had been an inveterate smoker of cigarettes. She would have time for a taste of the morning while he had his smoke. And if he returned and found her gone what mattered it? The inevitable beginning of conversations which she so dreaded would be put off for a time.

She never thought to come upon him standing thus alone, looking off at the beauty of the morning as if he enjoyed it. The sight of him held her still, watching, as his sleeping face had held her gaze earlier in the morning. How different he was from what she had expected! How the ten years had changed him! One could almost fancy it might have changed his spirit also—but for those letters—those terrible letters! The writer of those letters could not change, except for the worse!

And yet, he was handsome, intellectual looking, kindly in his bearing, appreciative of the beauty about him—she could not deny it. It was most astonishing. He had lost that baggy look under his eyes, and the weak, selfish, cruel pout of lip she remembered so keenly.

Then he turned, and a smile of delight and welcome lit up his face. In spite of herself, she could not keep an answering smile from glimmering faintly in her own.

"What! You up and out here?" he said, hastening closer to the step. "How are you feeling this morning? Better, I'm sure, or you would not be here so early."

"Oh, I had to get out to the air," she said. "I couldn't stand the car another minute. I wish we could walk the rest of the way."

"Do you?" he said, with a quick, surprised appreciation in his voice. "I was just wishing something like that myself. Do you see that beautiful straight road down there? I was longing to slide down this bank and walk over to that little village for breakfast. Then we could get an auto, perhaps, or a carriage, to take us on to another train. If you hadn't been so ill last night, I might have proposed it."

"Could we?" she asked, earnestly. "I should like it so much;" and there was eagerness in her voice. "What a lovely morning!" Her eyes were wistful, like the eyes of those who weep and wonder why they may not laugh, since sunshine is still yellow.

"Of course we could," he said, "if you were only able."

"Oh, I'm able enough. I should much rather do that than to go back into that stuffy car. But wouldn't they think it awfully queer of us to run away from the train this way?"

"They needn't know anything about it," he declared, like a boy about to play truant. "I'll slip back in the car and get our suit-cases. Is there anything of yours I might be in danger of leaving behind?"

"No, I put everything in my suit-case before I came out," she said, listlessly, as though she had already lost her desire to go.

"I'm afraid you are not able," he said, pausing solicitously as he scaled the steps.

She was surprised at his interest in her welfare.

"Why, of course I am," she said, insistently. "I have often taken longer walks than that looks to be, and I shall feel much better for being out. I really feel as if I couldn't stand it any longer in there."

"Good! Then, we'll try it!"

He hurried in the baggage and left her standing on the cinder roadbed beside the train looking off at the opening morning.

9

IT was just at that instant that the thick-set man in his berth not ten feet away became broadly conscious of the unwonted stillness of the train and the cessation of motion that had lulled him to such sound repose. So does a tiny, sharp sound strike upon our senses and bring them into life again from sleep, making us aware of a state of things that has been going on for some time perhaps without our realization. The sound that roused him may have been the click of the stateroom latch as Gordon opened the door.

The shades were down in the man's berth and the curtains drawn close. The daylight had not as yet penetrated through their thickness. But once awake his senses were immediately on the alert. He yawned, stretched and suddenly arrested another yawn to analyze the utter stillness all about him. A sonorous snore suddenly emphasized the quiet of the car, and made him aware of all the occupants of all those curtained apartments. His mind went over a quick résumé of the nights before, and detailed him at once to duty.

Another soft clicking of the latch set him to listening and his bristly shocked head was stuck instantly out between the curtains into the aisle, eyes toward the stateroom door, just in time to see that a man was stealing quietly down the passageway out of the end door, carrying two suit-cases and an umbrella. It was his man. He was sure instantly, and his mind grew frantic with the thought. Almost he had outdone himself through foolish sleep.

He half sprang from his berth, then remembered that he was but partly dressed, and jerked back quickly to grab his clothes, stopping in the operation of putting them on to yank up his window shade with an impatient click and flatten his face against the window-pane!

Yes, there they were down on the ground outside the train, both of them; man, woman, baggage and all slipping away from him while he slept peacefully and let them go! The language of his mind at that point was hot with invectives.

Gordon had made his way back to the girl's side without meeting any porters or wakeful fellow-passengers. But a distant rumbling greeted his ears. The waited-for express was coming. If they were to get away, it must be done at once or their flight would be discovered, and perhaps even prevented. It certainly was better not to have it known where they got off. He had taken the precaution to close the stateroom door behind him and so it might be some time before their absence would be discovered. Perhaps there would be other stops before the train reached Buffalo, in which case their track would not easily be followed. He had no idea that the evil eye of his pursuer was even then upon him.

Celia was already on the ground, looking off toward the little village wistfully. Just how it was to make her lot any brighter to get out of the train and run away to a strange little village she did not quite explain to herself, but it seemed to be a relief to her pent-up feelings. She was half afraid that George might raise some new objection when he returned.

Gordon swung himself down on the cinder path, scanning the track either way. The conductor and brakemen were not in sight. Far in the distance a black speck was rushing down upon them. Gordon could hear the vibration of the rail of the second track, upon which he placed his foot as he helped Celia across. In a moment more the train would pass. It was important that they should be down the embankment, out of sight. Would the delicate girl not be afraid of the steep incline?

She hesitated for just an instant at the top, for it was very steep. Then, looking up at him, she saw that he expected her to go down with him. She gave a little frightened gasp, set her lips, and started.

He held her as well as he could with two suitcases and an umbrella clutched in his other hand, and finally, as the grade grew steeper, he let go the baggage altogether, and it slid briskly down by itself, while he devoted himself to steadying the girl's now inevitable and swift descent.

It certainly was not an ideal way of travelling, this new style of "gravity" road, but it landed them without delay, though much shaken and scratched, and divested of every vestige of dignity. It was impossible not to laugh, and Celia's voice rang out merrily, showing that she had not always wept and looked sorrowful.

"Are you much hurt?" asked Gordon anxiously, holding her hands and looking down at her tenderly.

Before she could reply, the express train roared above them, drowning their voices and laughter; and when it was past they saw their own train take up its interrupted way grumblingly, and rapidly move off. If the passengers on those two trains had not been deeply wrapped in slumber, they might have been surprised to see two fashionably attired young persons, with hats awry and clasped hands, laughing in a country road at five o'clock of a May morning. But only one was awake, and by the time the two in the road below remembered to look up and take notice, the trains were rapidly disappearing.

The girl had been deeply impressed with Gordon's solicitude for her. It was so out of keeping with his letters. He had never seemed to care whether she suffered or not. In all the arrangements, he had said what *he* wanted, indeed what he *would have,* with an implied threat in the framing of his sentence in case she dared demur. Never had there been the least expression of desire for her happiness. Therefore it was something of a surprise to find him so gentle and thoughtful of her. Perhaps, after all, he would not prove so terrible to live with as she had feared. And yet—how could anyone who wrote those letters have any alleviating qualities? It could not be. She must harden herself against him. Still, if he would be outwardly decent to her, it would make her lot easier, of course.

But her course of mental reasoning was broken in upon by his stout denunications of himself.

"I ought not to have allowed you to slide down there," he declared. "It was terrible, after what you went through last night. I didn't realize how steep and rough it was. Indeed I didn't. I don't see how you ever can forgive me."

"Why, I'm not hurt," she said gently, astonished at his solicitation. There was a strange lump in her throat brought by his kindness, which threatened tears. Just why should kindness from an unexpected quarter bring tears?

"I'm only a little shaken up," she went on as she saw a real anxiety in his brown eyes, "and I don't mind it in the least. I think it was rather fun, don't you?"

A faint glimmer of a smile wavered over the corners of her mouth, and Gordon experienced a sudden desire to take her in his arms and kiss her. It was a strange new feeling. He had never had any such thought about Julia Bentley.

"Why, I—why, yes I guess so, if you're sure you're not hurt."

"Not a bit," she said, and then, for some unexplained reason, they both began to laugh. After that they felt better.

"If your shoes are as full of these miserable cinders as mine are, they need emptying," declared Gordon, shaking first one well-shod foot and then the other, and looking ruefully at the little velvet boots of the lady.

"Suppose you sit down"—he looked about for a seat, but the dewy grass was the only resting place visible. He pitched upon the suit-cases and improvised a chair. "Now, sit down and let me take them off for you."

He knelt in the road at her feet as she obeyed, protesting that she could do it for herself. But he overruled her, and began clumsily to unbutton the tiny buttons, holding the timid little foot firmly, almost reverently, against his knee.

He drew the velvet shoe softly off, and, turning it upside down, shook out the intruding cinders, put a clumsy finger in to make sure they were all gone; then shyly, tenderly, passed his hand over the sole of the fine silk-stockinged foot that rested so lightly on his knee, to make sure no cinders clung to it. The sight and touch of that little foot stirred him deeply. He had never before been called upon to render service so intimate to any woman, and he did it now with half-averted gaze and the utmost respect in his manner. As he did it he tried to speak about the morning, the departing train, the annoying cinders, anything to make their unusual position seem natural and unstrained. He felt deeply embarrassed, the more so because of his own double part in this queer masquerade.

Celia sat watching him, strangely stirred. Her wonder over his kindness grew with each moment, and her prejudices almost dissolved. She could not understand it. There must be something more he wanted of her, for George Hayne had never been kind in the past unless he wanted something of her. She dreaded lest she should soon find it out. Yet he did not look like a man who was deceiving her. She drew a deep sigh. If only it were true, and he were good and kind, and had never written those awful letters! How good and dear it would be to be tenderly cared for this way! Her lips drooped at the corners, and her eyelids drooped in company with the sigh; then Gordon looked up in great distress.

"You are tired!" he declared, pausing in his attempt to fasten the little pearl buttons. "I have been cruel to let you get off the train!"

"Indeed I'm not," said the girl, brightening with sudden effort. At least, she would not spoil the kindness while it lasted. It was surely better than what she had feared.

"You never can button those shoes with your fingers," she laughed, as he redoubled his efforts to capture a tiny disc of pearl and set it into its small velvet socket. "Here! I have a button-hook in my hand-bag. Try this."

She produced a small silver instrument from a gold-link bag on her arm and handed it to him. He took it helplessly, trying first one end and then the other, and succeeding with neither.

"Here, let me show you," she laughed, pulling off one glove. Her white fingers grasped the silver button-hook, and flashed in and out of the velvet holes, knitting the little shoe to the foot in no time. He watched the process in humble wonder, and she would not have been a human girl not to have been flattered with his interest and admiration. For the minute she forgot who and what he was, and let her laugh ring out merrily; and so with shy audacity he assayed to take off the other shoe.

They really felt quite well acquainted and as if they were going on a day's picnic, when they finally gathered up their belongings and started down the road. Gordon summoned all his ready wit and intellect to brighten the walk for her, though he found himself again and again on the brink of referring to his Washington life, or some other personal matter that would have brought a wondering question to her lips. He had decided that he must not tell her who he was until he could put her in an independent position, where she could get away from him at once if she chose. He was bound to look after her until he could place her in good hands, or at least where she could look after herself, and it was better to carry it out leaving her to think what she pleased until he could tell her everything. If all went well, they might be able to catch a Pittsburgh train that night and be in Washington the next day. Then, his message delivered, he would tell her the whole story. Until then he must hold his peace.

They went gaily down the road, the girl's pale cheeks beginning to flush with the morning and the exercise. She was not naturally delicate, and her faint the night before had been the result of a series of heavy strains on a heart burdened with terrible fear. The morning and his kindness had made her forget for the time that she was supposed to be walking into a world of dread and sacrifice.

> The year's at the spring,
> The day's at the morn

quoted Gordon gaily,

> Morning's at seven;
> The hill-side's dew-pearled —

He waved an umbrella off to where a hill flashed back a thousand lights from its jewelled grass-blades thickly set.

> The lark's on the wing;
> The snail's on the thorn

went on Celia suddenly catching his spirit, and pointing to a lark that darted up into the blue with a trill of the morning in his throat.

Gordon turned appreciative eyes upon her. It was good to have her take up his favorite poet in that tone of voice — a tone that showed she too knew and loved Browning.

> God's in his heaven,
> All's right with the world

finished Gordon in a quieter voice, looking straight into her eyes. "That seems very true, to-day, doesn't it?"

The blue eyes wavered with a hint of shadow in them as they looked back into the brown ones.

"Almost—perhaps," she faltered wistfully.

The young man wished he dared go behind that "almost—perhaps" and find out what she meant, but concluded it were better to bring back the smile and help her to forget for a little while at least.

Down by the brook they paused to rest, under a weeping willow, whose green-tinged plumes were dabbling in the brook. Gordon arranged the suitcases for her to sit upon, then climbed down to the brookside and gathered a great bunch of forget-me-nots, blue as her eyes, and brought them to her.

She looked at them in wonder, to think they grew out here, wild, untended. She had never seen them before, except in pots in the florist's windows. She touched them delicately with the tips of her fingers, as if they were too ethereal for earth; then fastened them in the breast of her gown.

"They exactly match your eyes!" he exclaimed involuntarily, and then wished he had not spoken, for she flushed and paled under his glance, until he felt he had been unduly bold. He wondered why he had said that. He never had been in the habit of saying pretty things to girls, but this girl somehow called it from him. It was genuine. He sat a moment abashed, not knowing what to say next, as if he were a shy boy, and she did not help him, for her eyelashes drooped in a long becoming sweep over her cheeks, and she seemed for the moment not to be able to carry off the situation. He was not sure if she were displeased or not.

Her heart had thrilled strangely as he spoke, and she was vexed with herself that it should be so. A man who had bullied and threatened her for three terrible months and forced her to marry him had no right to a thrill of her heart nor a look from her eyes, be he ever so kind for the moment. He certainly was nice and pleasant when he chose to be; she must watch herself, for never, never, must she yield weakly to his smooth overtures. Well did she know him. He had some reason for all this pleasantness. It would surely be revealed soon.

She stiffened her lips and tried to look away from him to the purple-green hills; but the echo of his words came upon her again, and again her heart thrilled at them. What if—oh what if he were all right, and she might accept the admiration in his voice? And yet how could that be possible? The sweet color came into her cheeks again, and the tears flew quickly to her eyes, till they looked all sky and dew, and she dared not turn back to him.

The silence remained unbroken, until a lark in the willow copse behind them burst forth into a song and broke the spell that was upon them.

"Are you offended at what I said?" he asked earnestly. "I am sorry if you did not like it. The words said themselves without my stopping to think whether you might not like it. Will you forgive me?"

"Oh," she said, lifting her forget-me-not eyes to his, "I am not offended. There is nothing to forgive. It was—beautiful!"

Then his eyes spoke the compliment over again, and the thrill started anew in her heart, till her cheeks grew quite rosy, and she buried her face in the coolness of the tiny flowers to hide her confusion.

"It was very true," he said in a low, lover-like voice that sounded like a caress.

"Oughtn't we to hurry on to catch our train?" said Celia, suddenly springing to her feet. "I'm quite rested now." She felt if she stayed there another moment she would yield to the spell he had cast upon her.

With a dull thud of consciousness the man got himself to his feet and reminded himself that this was another man's promised wife to whom he had been letting his soul go out.

"Don't let anything hinder you! Don't let anything hinder you!" suddenly babbled out of the little brook, and he gathered up his suit-cases and started on.

"I am going to carry my suit-case," declared a very decided voice behind him, and a small hand seized hold of its handle.

"I beg your pardon, you are not!" declared Gordon in a much more determined voice.

"But they are too heavy for you—both of them—and the umbrella too," she protested. "Give me the umbrella then."

But he would not give her even the umbrella, rejoicing in his strength to shield her and bear her burdens. As she walked beside him, she remembered vividly a morning when George Hayne had made her carry two heavy baskets, that his hands might be free to shoot birds. Could this be the same George Hayne?

Altogether, it was a happy walk, and far shorter than either had expected it to be, though Gordon worried not a little about his frail companion before they came to the outskirts of the village, and kept begging her to sit down and rest again, but she would not. She was quite eager and excited about the strange village to which they were coming. Its outlying farm-houses were all so clean and white, with green blinds folded placidly over their front windows and only their back doors astir. The cows all looked peaceful, and the dogs all seemed friendly.

They walked up the village street, shaded in patches with flecks of sunshine through the young leaves. If anyone had told Celia Hathaway the night before that she would have walked and talked thus to-day with her bridegroom she would have laughed him to scorn. But now all unconsciously she had drifted into an attitude of friendliness with the man whom she had thought to hate all the rest of her life.

One long, straight, maple-lined street, running parallel to the stream, comprised the village. They walked to the centre of it, and still saw no signs of a restaurant. A post-office, a couple of stores and a bakery made up the business portion of the town, and upon enquiry it appeared that there was no public eating house, the one hotel of the place having been sold at auction the week before on account of the death of the owner. The early village loungers stared disinterestedly at the phenomenal appearance in their midst of a couple of city folks with their luggage and no apparent means of transit except their two delicately shod feet. It presented a problem too grave to be solved unassisted, and there were solemn shakings of the head over them. At last one who had discouragingly stated the village lack of a public inn asked casually:

"Hed a runaway?"

"Oh, no!" laughed Gordon pleasantly. "We didn't travel with horses."

"Hed a puncture, then," announced the village wise-acre, shifting from one foot to the other.

"Wal, you come the wrong direction to git help," said another languid listener. "Thur ain't no garridge here. The feller what uset to keep it skipped out with Sam Galt's wife a month ago. You'd ought to 'a' turned back to Ashville. They got a good blacksmith there can tinker ye up."

"Is that so?" said Gordon interestedly. "Well now that's too bad, but perhaps as it can't be helped we'll have to forget it. What's the next town on ahead and how far?"

"Sugar Grove's two mile further on, and Milton's five. They've got a garridge and a rest'rant to Milton, but that's only sence the railroad built a junction there."

"Has any one here a conveyance I could hire to take us to Milton?" questioned Gordon, looking anxiously about the indolent group.

"I wouldn't want to drive to Milton for less'n five dollars," declared a lazy youth after a suitable pause.

"Very well," said Gordon. "How soon can you be ready, and what sort of a rig have you? Will it be comfortable for the lady?"

The youth eyed the graceful woman in her dainty city dress scornfully. His own country lass was dressed far prettier to his mind; but the eyes of her, so blue, like the little weed-flowers at her breast, went to his head. His tongue was suddenly tied.

"It's all right! It's as good's you'll get!" volunteered a sullen-faced man half sitting on a sugar barrel. He was of a type who preferred to see fashionable ladies uncomfortable.

The youth departed for his "team" and after some enquiries Gordon found that he might be able to persuade the owner of the tiny white colonial cot across the street to prepare a "snack" for himself and his companion, so they went across the street and waited fifteen minutes in a dank little hair-cloth parlor adorned in funeral wreaths and knit tidies, for a delicious breakfast of poached eggs, coffee, home-made bread, butter like roses, and a comb of amber honey. To each the experience was a new one, and they enjoyed it together like two children, letting their eyes speak volumes of comments in the midst of the old lady's volubility. Unconsciously by their experiences they were being brought into sympathy with each other.

The "rig" when it arrived at the door driven by the blushing youth proved to be a high spring-wagon with two seats. In the front one the youth lounged without a thought of assisting his passengers. Gordon swung the baggage up, and then lifted the girl into the back seat, himself taking the place behind her, and planting a firm hand and arm behind the backless seat, that she might feel more secure.

That ride, with his arm behind her, was just one more link in the pretty chain of sympathy that was being welded about these two. Unconsciously more and more she began to droop, until when she grew very tired he seemed to know at once.

"Just lean against my arm," he said. "You must be very tired and it will help you bear the jolting." He spoke as if his arm were made of wood or iron, and was merely one of his belongings, like an umbrella or suit-case. He made it seem quite the natural thing for her to lean against him. If he had claimed it as her right and privilege as wife, she would have recoiled from him for recalling to her the hated relation, and would have sat straight as a bean-pole the rest of the way, but, as it was, she sank back a trifle deprecatingly, and realized that it was a great help. In her heart she thanked him for making it possible for her to rest without entirely compromising her attitude toward him. There was nothing about it that suggested anything loverlike; it seemed just a common courtesy.

Yet the strong arm almost trembled as he felt the precious weight against it, and he wished that the way were ten miles instead of five. Once, as Celia leaned forward to point to a particularly lovely bit of view that opened up as they wound around a curve in the road, they ran over a stone, and the wagon gave an unexpected jolt. Gordon reached his hand out to steady her, and she settled back to his arm with a sense of safety and being cared for that was very pleasant. Looking up shyly, she saw his eyes upon her, with that deep look of admiration and something more, and again that strange thrill of joy that had come when he gave her the forget-me-nots swept through her. She felt almost as if she were harboring a sinful thought when she remembered the letters he had written; but the joy of the day, and the sweetness of happiness for even a moment, when she had been for so long a time sad, was so pleasant that she let herself enjoy it and drift, refusing to think evil of him now, here, in this bright day. Thus like children on a picnic, they passed through Sugar Grove and came to the town of Milton, and there they bade their driver good-by, rewarding him with a crisp five-dollar bill. He drove home with a vision of smiles in forget-me-not eyes, and a marked inability to tell anything about his wonderful passengers who had filled the little village with awe and amazement, and had given no clue to anyone as to who or what they were.

10

BUT to go back to the pursuer, in his berth, baffled and frantic and raging. With hands that fumbled because of their very eagerness he sought to get into his garments, and find his shoes from the melée of blankets and other articles in the berth, all the time keeping one eye out of the window, for he must not let his prey get away from him now. He must watch and see what they were going to do. How fortunate that he had wakened in time for that. At least he would have a clue. Where was this? A station?

He stopped operations once more to gaze off at the landscape, a desolate country scene to his city hardened eyes. Not a house in sight, nor a station. The spires of the distant village seemed like a mirage to him. This couldn't be a station. What were those two doing down there anyway? Dared he risk calling the conductor and having him hold them? No, this affair must be kept absolutely quiet. Mr. Holman had said that if a breath of the matter came out it was worse than death for all concerned. He must just get off this train as fast as he could and follow them if they were getting away. It might be he could get the man in a lonely place—it would be easy enough to watch his chance and gag the lady—he had done such things before. He felt far more at home in such an affair than he had the night before at the Holman dinner table. What a pity one of the others had not come along. It would be mere child's play for two to handle those two who looked as if they would turn frightened at the first threat. However, he felt confident that he could manage the affair alone.

He panted with haste and succeeded in getting the wrong legs into his trousers and having to begin all over again, his efforts greatly hampered by the necessity for watching out the window.

Then came the distant rumble of an oncoming train, and an answering scream from his own engine. The two on the ground had crossed quickly over the second track and were looking down the steep embankment. Were they going down there? What fate that he was not ready to follow them at once! The train that was coming would pass — their own would start — and he could not get out. His opportunity was going from him and he could not find his shoes!

Well what of it? He would go without! What were shoes at a time like this? Surely he could get along barefoot, and beg a pair at some farmhouse, or buy a pair at a country store. He must get out at any cost, shoes or no shoes. Grasping his coat which contained his money and valuables he sprang from his berth straight into the arms of the porter who was hurrying back to his car after having been out to gossip with a brakeman over the delay.

"What's de mattah, sah?" asked the astonished porter, rallying quickly from the shock and assuming his habitual courtesy.

"My shoes!" roared the irate traveller. "What have you done with my shoes?"

"Quiet, sah, please sah, you'll wake de whole cyah," said the porter. "I put yoh shoes under de berth sah, righ whar I allus puts 'em aftah blackin' sah."

The porter stooped and extracted the shoes from beneath

the curtain and the traveller, whose experience in Pullmans was small, grabbed them furiously and made for the door, shoes in hand, for with a snort and a lurch and a preliminary jar the train had taken up its motion, and a loud rushing outside proclaimed that the other train was passing.

The porter, feeling that he had been treated with injustice, stood gazing reproachfully after the man for a full minute before he followed him to tell him that the wash-room was at the other end of the car and not down past the drawing-room as he evidently supposed.

He found his man standing in stocking feet on the cold iron platform, his head out of the opening left in the vestibuled train, for when the porter came in he had drawn shut the outer door and slammed down the movable platform, making it impossible for anyone to get out. There was only the little opening the size of a window above the grating guard, and the man clung to it as if he would jump over it if he only dared. He was looking back over the track and his face was not good to see.

He turned wildly upon the porter.

"I want you to stop this train and let me off," he shouted. "I've lost something valuable back there on the track. Stop the train quick, I tell you or I'll sue the railroad."

"What was it you lost?" asked the porter respectfully. He wasn't sure but the man was half asleep yet.

"It was a—my—why it was a very valuable paper. It means a fortune to me and several other people and I must go back and get it. Stop the train, I tell you, at once or I'll jump out."

"I can't stop de train sah, you'll hev to see de conductah sah, 'bout dat. But I specks there's mighty little prospec' o' gettin' dis train stopped foh it gits to its destinashun sah. We's one hour a'hind time now, sah, an' he's gotta make up foh we gets to Buff 'lo."

The excited passenger railed and stormed until several sleepers were awakened and stuck curious sleepy countenances out from the curtains of their berths, but the porter was obdurate, and would not take any measures to stop the train, nor even call the conductor until the passenger promised to return quietly to his berth.

The thick-set man was not used to obeying but he saw that he was only hindering himself and finally hurried back to his berth where he hastily parted the curtains, craning his neck to see back along the track and over the green valley growing smaller and smaller now in the distance. He could just make out two moving specks on the white winding ribbon of the road. He felt sure he knew the direction they were taking. If he only could get off that train he could easily catch them, for they would have no idea he was coming, and would take no precautions. If he had only wakened a few seconds sooner he would have been following them even now.

Fully ten minutes he argued with the conductor, showing a wide incongruity between his language and his gentlemanly attire, but the conductor would do nothing but promise to let him down at a water tower ten miles ahead where they had to slow up for water. He said sue or no sue he had his orders, and the thick-set man did not inspire him either to sympathy or confidence. The conductor had been many years on the road and generally knew when to stop his train and when to let it go on.

Sullenly the thick-set man accepted the conductor's decision and prepared to leave the train at the water tower, his eye out for the landmarks along the way as he completed his hasty toilet.

He was in no pleasant frame of mind, having missed a goodly amount of his accustomed stimulants the night before, and seeing little prospect of either stimulants or breakfast before him. He was not built for a ten-mile walk over the cinders and his flabby muscles already ached at the prospect. But then, of course he would not have to go far before he found an automobile or some kind of conveyance to help him on his way. He looked eagerly from the window for indications of garages or stables, but the river wound its silver way among the gray green willow fringes, and the new grass shone a placid emerald plan with nothing more human than a few cows grazing here and there. Not even a horse that might be borrowed without his owner's knowledge. It was a strange, forsaken spot, ten whole miles and no sign of any public livery! Off to the right and left he could see villages, but they were most of them too far away from the track to help him any. It began to look as if he must just foot it all the way. Now and then a small shanty or tiny dwelling whizzed by near at hand, but nothing that would relieve his situation.

It occurred to him to go into the dining car for breakfast, but even as he thought of it the conductor told him that the train would stop in two minutes and he must be ready to get off, for they did not stop long.

He certainly looked a harmless creature, that thick-set man as he stood alone upon the cinder elevation and surveyed the landscape o'er. Ten miles from his quarry, alone on a stretch of endless ties and rails with a gleaming river mocking him down in the valley, and a laughing sky jeering overhead. He started down the shining track his temper a wreck, his mind in chaos, his soul at war with the world. The worst of it all was that the whole fault was his own for going to sleep. He began to fear that he had lost his chance. Then he set his ugly jaw and strode ahead.

The morning sun poured down upon the thick-set man on his pilgrimage, and waxed hotter until noon. Trains whizzed mercilessly by and gave him no succor. Weary, faint, and fiercely thirsty he came at last to the spot where he was satisfied his quarry had escaped. He could see the marks of their rough descent in the steep cinder bank, and assaying the same himself came upon a shred of purple silk caught on a bramble at the foot.

Puffing and panting, bruised and foot-sore, he sat down at the very place where Celia had stopped to have her shoes fastened, and mopped his purple brow, but there was triumph in his ugly eye, and after a few moment's rest he trudged onward. That town over there ought to yield both conveyance and food as well as information concerning those he sought. He would catch them. They could never get away from him. He was on their track again, though hours behind. He would get them yet and no man should take his reward from him.

Almost spent he came at last to the village, and ate a surprisingly large dish of beef and vegetable stew at the quaint little house where Celia and Gordon had breakfasted, but the old lady who served it to them was shy about talking, and though admitting that a couple of people had been there that morning she was noncommittal about their appearance. They might have been young and good-looking and worn feathers in their hats, and they might not. She wasn't one for noticing people's appearance if they treated her civilly and paid their bills. Would he have another cup of coffee? He would, and also two more pieces of pie, but he got very little further information.

It was over at the corner store where he finally went in search of something stronger than coffee that he further pursued his investigations.

The loungers were still there. It was their only business in life and they were most diligent in it. They eyed the newcomer with relish and settled back on their various barrels and boxes to enjoy whatever entertainment the gods were about to provide to relieve their monotonous existence.

A house divided against itself cannot stand. This man's elegant garments assumed for the nonce did not fit the rest of his general appearance which had been accentuated by his long, hot, dusty tramp. The high evening hat was jammed on the back of his head and bore a decided dent where it had rolled down the cinder embankment, his collar was wilted and lifeless, his white laundered tie at half mast, his coat awry, and his fine patent leather shoes which pinched were covered with dust and had caused a limp like the hardest tramp upon the road. Moreover, again the speech of the man betrayed him, and the keen-minded old gossips who were watching him suspiciously sized him up at once the minute he opened his mouth.

"Saw anything of a couple of young folks walking down this way?" he enquired casually, pausing to light a cigar with which he was reinforcing himself for further travel.

One man allowed that there might have passed such people that day. He hardly seemed willing to commit himself, but another vouchsafed the information that "Joe here driv two parties of thet description to Milton this mornin'—jes' got back. Mebbe he could answer fer 'em."

Joe frowned. He did not like the looks of the thick-set man. He still remembered the forget-me-not eyes.

But the stranger made instant request to be driven to Milton, offering ten dollars for the same when he found that his driver was reluctant, and that Milton was a railroad centre. A few keen questions had made him sure that his man had gone to Milton.

Joe haggled, allowed his horse was tired, and he didn't care about the trip twice in one day, but finally agreed to take the man for fifteen dollars, and sauntered off to get a fresh horse. He had no mind to be in a hurry. He had his own opinion about letting those two "parties" get out of the way before the third put in an appearance, but he had no mind to lose fifteen dollars. It would help to buy the ring he coveted for his girl.

In due time Joe rode leisurely up and the impatient traveller climbed into the high spring wagon and was driven away from the apathetic gaze of the country loungers who unblinkingly took in the fact that Joe was headed toward Ashville, and evidently intended taking his fare to Milton by way of that village, a thirty-mile drive at least. The man would get the worth of his money in ride. A grim twinkle sat in their several eyes as the spring wagon turned the curve in the road and was lost to sight, and after due silence an old stager spoke:

"Do you reckon that there was their sho-fur?" he requested languidly.

"Naw!" replied a farmer's son vigorously. "He wouldn't try to showf all dolled up like that. He's the rich dad comin' after the runaways. Joe didn't intend he shell get 'em yet awhile. I reckon the ceremony'll be over 'fore he steps in to interfere." This lad went twice a month to Milton to the "movies" and was regarded as an authority on matters of romance. A pause showed that his theory had taken root in the minds of his auditors.

"Wal, I reckon Joe thinks the longest way round is the shortest way home," declared the old stager. "Joe never did like them cod-fish swells—but how do you 'count fer the style o' that gal? She wasn't like her dad one little bit."

"Oh, she's ben to collidge I 'spose," declared the youth. "They get all that off'n collidge."

"Serves the old man right fer sendin' his gal to a fool collidge when she ought to ben home learnin' to house-keep. I hope she gits off with her young man all right," said a grim old lounger, and a cackle of laughter went round the group, which presently broke up, for this had been a strenuous day and all felt their need of rest; besides they wanted to get home and tell the news before some neighbor got ahead of them.

All this time Celia and Gordon were touring Milton, serenely unconscious of danger near, or guardian angel of the name of Joe.

Investigation disclosed the fact that there was a train for Pittsburgh about three in the afternoon. Gordon sent a code telegram to his chief, assuring him of the safety of the message, and of his own intention to proceed to Washington as fast as steam could carry him. Then he took the girl to a restaurant, where they mounted two high stools, and partook with an unusually ravenous appetite of nearly everything on

the menu—corn soup, roast beef, baked trout, stewed toma-
toes, cole slaw, custard, apple, and mince pies, with a cup of
good country coffee and real cream—all for twenty-five
cents apiece.

It was a very merry meal. Celia felt somehow as if for the
time all memory of the past had been taken from her, and
she were free to think and act happily in the present, without any great problems to solve or decisions to make. Just
two young people off having a good time, they were, at least
until that afternoon train came.

After their dinner, they took a short walk to a tiny park
where two white ducks disported themselves on a seven-by-
nine pond, spanned by a rustic bridge where lovers had cut
their initials. Gordon took out his knife and idly cut C. H.
in the rough bark of the upper rail, while his companion sat
on the little board seat and watched him. She was ponder-
ing over the fact that he had cut her initials, and not his own.
It would have been like the George of old to cut his own and
never once think of hers. And he had put but one H. Probably he thought of her now as Celia Hayne, without the
Hathaway, or else he was so used to writing her name Celia
Hathaway, that he was not thinking at all.

Those letters! How they haunted her and clouded every
bright experience that she fain would have grasped and held
for a little hour.

They were silent now, while he worked and she thought.
He had finished the C. H., and was cutting another C, but
instead of making another H, he carefully carved out the letter G. What was that for? C. G.? Who was C. G.? Oh, how
stupid! George, of course. He had started a C by mistake.
But he did not add the expected H. Instead he snapped his
knife shut, laid his hand over the carving, and leaned over
the rail.

"Some time, perhaps, we'll come here again, and remember," he said, and then bethought him that he had no right
to hope for any such anniversary.

"Oh!" She looked up into his eyes, startled, troubled, the haunting of her fears in the shadows of the blue.

He looked down into them and read her trouble, read and understood, and looked back his great desire to comfort her.

His look carried further than he meant it should. For the third time that day a thrill of wonder and delight passed over her and left her fearful with a strange joy that she felt she should put from her.

It was only an instant, that look, but it brought the bright color to both faces, and made Gordon feel the immediate necessity of changing the subject.

"See those little fishes down there," he said pointing to the tiny lake below them.

Through a blur of tears, the girl looked down and saw the tiny, sharp-finned creatures darting here and there in a beam of sun like a small search-light set to show them off.

She moved her hand on the rail to lean further over, and her soft fingers touched his hand for a moment. She would not draw them away quickly, lest she hurt him; why, she did not know, but she could not—would not—hurt him. Not now! The two hands lay side by side for a full minute, and the touch to Gordon was as if a roseleaf had kissed his soul. He had never felt anything sweeter. He longed to gather the little hand into his clasp and feel its pulses trembling there as he had felt it in the church the night before, but she was not his. He might not touch her till she had her choice of what to do, and she would never choose him, never, when she knew how he had deceived her.

That one supreme moment they had of perfect consciousness, consciousness of the drawing of the soul to soul, of the sweetness of that hovering touch of hands, of the longing to know and understand each other.

Then a sharp whistle sounded, and a farmer's boy with a new rake and a sack of corn on his shoulder came sauntering briskly down the road to the bridge. Instantly they drew

apart, and Celia felt that she had been on the verge of disloyalty to her true self.

They walked silently back to the station, each busy with
his own thoughts, each conscious of that one moment when
the other had come so near.

THERE were a lot of people at the station. They had been to a family gathering of some sort from their remarks, and they talked loudly and much, so that the two stood apart—for the seats were all occupied—and had no opportunity for conversation, save a quiet smiling comment now and then upon the chatter about them, or the odd remarks they heard.

There had come a constraint upon them, a withdrawing of each into his shell, each conscious of something that separated. Gordon struggled to prevent it, but he seemed helpless. Celia would smile in answer to his quiet remarks, but it was a smile of distance, such as she had worn early in the morning. She had quite found her former standing ground, with its fence of prejudice, and she was repairing the breaks through which she had gone over to the enemy during the day. She was bracing herself with dire reminders, and snatches from those terrible letters which were written in characters of fire in her heart. Never, never, could she care for a man who had done what this man had done. She had forgotten for a little while those terrible things he had said of her dear dead father. How could she have forgotten for an instant! How could she have let her hand lie close to the hand that had defiled itself by writing such things!

By the time they were seated in the train, she was freezing in her attitude, and poor Gordon sat miserably beside her and tried to think what he had done to offend her. It was not his fault that her hand had lain near his on the rail. She had put it there herself. Perhaps she expected him to put his over it, to show her that he cared as a bridegroom should care — as he did care, in reality, if he only had the right. And perhaps she was hurt that he had stood coolly and said or done nothing. But he could not help it.

Much to Gordon's relief, the train carried a parlor car, and it happened on this particular day to be almost deserted save for a deaf old man with a florid complexion and a gold-knobbed cane who slumbered audibly at the further end from the two chairs Gordon selected. He established his companion comfortably, disposed of the baggage, and sat down, but the girl paid no heed to him. With a sad, set face, she stared out of the window, her eyes seeming to see nothing. For two hours she sat so, he making remarks occasionally, to which she made little or no reply, until he lapsed into silence, looking at her with troubled eyes. Finally, just as they neared the outskirts of Pittsburgh, he leaned softly forward and touched her coat-sleeve, to attract her attention.

"Have I offended — hurt — you in any way?" he asked gently. She turned toward him, and her eyes were brimming full of tears.

"No," she said, and her lips were trembling. "No, you have been — most — kind — but — but I cannot forget *those letters!*" She ended with a sob and put up her handkerchief quickly to stifle it.

"Letters?" he asked helplessly. "What letters?"

"The letters you wrote me. All the letters of the last five months. I cannot forget them. I can *never* forget them! How could you *think* I could?"

He looked at her anxiously, not knowing what to say, and yet he must say something. The time had come when some kind of an understanding, some clearing up of facts, must take place. He must go cautiously, but he must find out what was the matter. He could not see her suffer so. There must be some way to let her know that so far as he was concerned she need suffer nothing further and that he would do all in his power to set her right with her world.

But letters! He had written no letters. His face lighted up with the swift certainty of one thing about which he had not dared to be sure. She still thought him the man she had intended to marry. She was not therefore troubled about that phase of the question. It was strange, almost unbelievable, but it was true that he personally was not responsible for the trouble in her eyes. What trouble she might feel when she knew all, he had yet to find out, but it was a great relief to be sure of so much. Still, something must be said.

"Letters!" he repeated again stupidly, and then added with perplexed tone: "Would you mind telling me just what it was in the letters that hurt you?"

She turned eyes of astonishment on him.

"How can you ask?" she said almost bitterly. "You surely must know how terrible they were to me! You could not be the man you have seemed to be to-day if you did not know what you were doing to me in making all those terrible threats. You must know how cruel they were."

"I am afraid I don't understand," he said earnestly, the trouble still most apparent in his eyes, "Would you mind being a little more explicit? Would you mind telling me exactly what you think I wrote you that sounded like a threat?"

He asked the question half hesitatingly, because he was not quite sure whether he was justified in thus obtaining private information under false pretenses, and yet he felt that he must know just what troubled her or he could never help her, and he was sure that if she knew he was an utter stranger, even a kindly one, those gentle lips would never open to inform him upon her torturer. As it was she could tell him her trouble with a perfectly clear conscience, thinking she was telling it to the man who knew all about it. But his hesitation about prying into an utter stranger's private affairs, even with a good motive, gave him an air of troubled dignity, and real anxiety to know his fault that puzzled the girl more than all that had gone before.

"I cannot understand how you can ask such a question, since it has been the constant subject of discussion in all our letters!" she replied, sitting up with asperity and drying her tears. She was on the verge of growing angry with him for his petty, wilful misunderstanding of words whose meaning she felt he must know well.

"I do ask it," he said quietly, "and, believe me, I have a good motive in doing so."

She looked at him in surprise. It was impossible to be angry with those kindly eyes, even though he did persist in a wilful stupidity.

"Well, then, since you wish it stated once more I will tell you," she declared, the tears welling again into her eyes. "You first demanded that I marry you — demanded — without any pretense whatever of caring for me — with a hidden threat in your demand that if I did not, you would bring some dire calamity upon me by means that were already in your power. You took me for the same foolish little girl whom you had delighted to tease for years before you went abroad to live. And when I refused you, you told me that you could not only take away from my mother all the property which she had inherited from her brother, by means of a will made just before my uncle's death, and unknown except to his lawyer and you; but that you could and would blacken my dear dead father's name and honor, and show that every cent that belonged to Mother and Jefferson and myself was stolen property. When I challenged you to prove any such thing against my honored father, you went still further and threatened to bring out a terrible story and prove it with witnesses who would swear to anything you said. You knew my father's white life, you as much as owned your charges were false, and yet you dared to send me a letter from a vile creature who pretended that she was his first wife, and who said she could prove that he had spent much of his time in her company. You knew the whole thing was a falsehood, but you dared to threaten to make this known throughout the newspapers if I did not marry you. You realized that I knew that, even though few people and no friends would believe such a thing of my father, such a report in the papers—false though it was—would crush my mother to death. You knew that I would give my life to save her, and so you had me in your power, as you have me now. You have always wanted me in your power, just because you love to torture, and now you have me. But you cannot make me forget what you have done. I have given my life but I cannot give any more. If it is not sufficient you will have to do your worst."

She dropped her face into the little wet handkerchief, and Gordon sat with white, drawn countenance and clenched hands. He was fairly trembling with indignation toward the villain who had thus dared impose upon this delicate flower of womanhood. He longed to search the world over for the false bridegroom; and, finding, give him his just dues.

And what should he do or say? Dared he tell her at once who he was and trust to her kind heart to forgive his terrible blunder and keep his secret till the message was safely delivered? Dared he? Had he any right? No, the secret was not his to divulge either for his own benefit or for any other's. He must keep that to himself. But he must help her in some way.

At last he began to speak, scarcely knowing what he was about to say:

"It is terrible, *terrible*, what you have told me. To have written such things to one like you—in fact, to any one on earth—seems to me unforgivable. It is the most inhuman cruelty I have ever heard of. You are fully justified in hating and despising the man who wrote such words to you."

"Then, why did you write them?" she burst forth. "And how can you sit there calmly and talk that way about it, as if you had nothing to do with the matter?"

"Because I never wrote those letters," he said, looking her steadily, earnestly, in the eyes.

"You never wrote them!" she exclaimed excitedly. "You dare to deny it?"

"I dare to deny it." His voice was quiet, earnest, convincing.

She looked at him, dazed, bewildered, indignant, sorrowful. "But you cannot deny it," she said, her fragile frame trembling with excitement. "I have the letters all in my suit-case. You cannot deny your own handwriting. I have the last awful one — the one in which you threatened Father's good name — here in my hand-bag. I dared not put it with the rest, and I had no opportunity to destroy it before leaving home. I felt as if I must always keep it with me, lest otherwise its awful secret would somehow get out. There it is. Read it and see your own name signed to the words you say you did not write!"

While she talked, her trembling fingers had taken a folded, crumpled letter from her little handbag, and this she reached over and laid upon the arm of his chair.

"Read it," she said. "Read it and see that you cannot deny it."

"I should rather not read it," he said. "I do not need to read it to deny that I ever wrote such things to you."

"But I insist that you read it," said the girl.

"If you insist I will read it," he said, taking the letter reluctantly and opening it.

She sat watching him furtively through the tears while he read, saw the angry flush steal into his cheeks as the villainy of a fellow man was revealed to him through the brief, coarse, cruel epistle, and she mistook the flush for one of shame.

Then his true brown eyes looked up and met her tearful gaze steadily, a fine anger burning in them.

"And you think I wrote that?" he said, a something in his voice she could not understand.

"What else could I think? It bears your signature," she answered coldly.

"The letter is vile," he said, "and the man who wrote is a blackguard, and deserves the utmost that the law allows for such offenses. With your permission, I shall make it my business to see that he gets it."

"What do you mean?" she said, wide-eyed. "How could you punish yourself? You cannot still deny that you wrote the letter."

"I still deny that I wrote it, or ever saw it until you handed it to me just now."

The girl looked at him, nonplussed, more than half convinced, in spite of reason.

"But isn't that your handwriting?"

"It is not. Look!"

He took out his fountain pen, and holding the letter on the arm of her chair, he wrote rapidly in his natural hand her own name and address beneath the address on the envelope, then held it up to her.

"Do they look alike?"

The two writings were as utterly unlike as possible, the letter being addressed in an almost unreadable scrawl, and the fresh writing standing fine and clear, in a script that spoke of character and business ability. Even a child could see at a glance that the two were not written by the same hand — and yet of course, it might have been practised for the purpose of deception. This thought flashed through the minds of both even as he held it out for her to look.

She looked from the envelope to his eyes and back to the letter, startled, not knowing what to think.

But before either of them had time for another word the conductor, the porter, and several people from the car behind came hurriedly through, and they realized that while they talked the train had come to a halt, amid the blazing electric lights of a great city station.

"Why," said Gordon startled, "we must have reached Pittsburgh. Is this Pittsburgh?" he called out to the vanishing porter.

"Yas sah!" yelled the porter, putting his head around the curve of the passageway. "You bettah hurry sah, foh dis train goes on to Cincinnati pretty quick. We's late gittin' in you see."

Neither of them had noticed a man in rough clothes with slouch hat and hands in his pockets who had boarded the train a few miles back and walked through the car several times eyeing them keenly. He stuck his head in at the door now furtively and drew back quickly again out of sight.

Gordon hurriedly gathered up the baggage, and they went out of the car, the porter rushing back as they reached the door, to assist them and get a last tip. There was no opportunity to say anything more, as they mingled with the crowd, until the porter landed their baggage in the great station and hurried back to his train. The man with the slouch hat followed and stood unobtrusively behind them.

Gordon looked down at the white, drawn face of the girl, and his heart was touched with compassion for her trouble. He must make her some satisfactory explanation at once that would set her heart at rest, but he could not do it here, for every seat about them was filled with noisy chattering folk. He stooped and whispered low and tenderly:

"Don't worry, little girl! Just try to trust me, and I will explain it all."

"Can you explain it?" she asked anxiously, as if catching at a rope thrown out to save her life.

"Perfectly," he said, "if you will be patient and trust me. But we cannot talk here. Just wait in this seat until I see if I can get the stateroom on the sleeper."

He left her with his courteous bow, and she sat watching

his tall, fine figure as he threaded his way among the crowds to the Pullman window, her heart filled with mingling emotions. In spite of her reason, a tiny bit of hope for the future was springing up in her heart and without her own will she found herself inclined to trust him. At least it was all she could do at present.

12

BACK at Milton an hour before, when the shades of dusk were falling and a slender moon hung timidly on the edge of the horizon, a horse drawing a spring wagon ambled deliberately into town and came to a reluctant halt beside the railroad station, having made a wide detour through the larger part of the country on the way to that metropolis.

The sun had been hot, the road much of it rough, and the jolts over stones and bumps had not added to the comfort of the thick-set man, already bruised and weary from his travels. Joe's conversation had not ceased. He had given his guest a wide range of topics, discoursing learnedly on the buckwheat crop and the blight that might be expected to assail the cherry trees. He pointed out certain portions of land infested with rattlesnakes, and told blood-curdling stories of experiences with stray bears and wild cats in a maple grove through which they passed till the passenger looked furtively behind him and urged the driver to hurry a little faster.

Joe, seeing his gullibility, only made his stories of country life the bigger, for the thick-set man, though bold as a lion in his own city haunts, was a coward in the unknown world of the country.

When the traveller looking at his watch urged Joe to make haste and asked how many miles further Milton was, Joe managed it that the horse should stumble on a particularly stony bit of road. Then getting down gravely from the wagon he examined the horse's feet each in turn, shaking his head sadly over the left fore foot.

"Jes' 'z I 'sposed," he meditated dreamily. "Stone bruise! Lame horse! Don't believe I ought to go on. Sorry, but it'll be ruination of the horse. You ain't in a hurry I hope."

The passenger in great excitement promised to double the fare if the young man would get another horse and hurry him forward, and after great professions of doubt Joe gave in and said he would try the horse, but it wouldn't do to work him hard. They would have to let him take his time. He couldn't on any account leave the horse behind anywhere and get a fresh one because it belonged to his best friend and he promised to bring it back safe and sound. They would just take their time and go slow and see if the horse could stand it. He wouldn't think of trying it if it weren't for the extra money which he needed.

So the impatient traveller was dragged fuming along weary hour after weary hour through the monotonous glory of a spring afternoon of which he saw nothing but the dust of the road as he tried to count the endless miles. Every mile or two Joe would descend from the wagon seat and fuss around with the horse's leg, the horse nothing loth at such unprecedented attention dozing cozily by the roadside during the process. And so was the traveller brought to his destination ten minutes after the last train that stopped at Milton that night had passed the station.

The telegraph office was not closed however, and without waiting to haggle, the passenger paid his thirty dollars for the longest journey he ever took, and disappeared into the station, while Joe, whipping up his petted animal, and whistling cherrily:

"Where did you get that girl—"

went rattling down the short cut from Milton home at a surprising pace for a lame horse. He was eating his supper at home in a little more than an hour, and the horse seemed to have miraculously recovered from his stone bruise. Joe was wondering how his girl would look in a hat with purple plumes, and thinking of his thirty dollars with a chuckle.

It was surprising how much that thick-set man, weary and desperate though he was, could accomplish, when once he reached the telegraph station and sent his messages flying on their way. In less than three minutes after his arrival he had extracted from the station agent the fact that two people, man and woman, answering the description he gave, had bought tickets for Pittsburgh and taken the afternoon train for that city. The agent had noticed them on account of their looking as if they came from the city. He especially noticed the purple plumes, the like of which he had never seen before. He had taken every minute he could get off from selling tickets and sending telegrams to watch the lady through his little cobwebby window. They didn't wear hats like that in Milton.

In ten minutes one message was on its way to a crony in Pittsburgh with whom the thick-set man kept in constant touch for just such occasions as the present, stirring him to strenuous action; another message had winged its mysterious way to Mr. Holman, giving him the main facts in the case; while a third message caught another crony thirty miles north of Pittsburgh and ordered him to board the evening express at his own station, hunt up the parties described, and shadow them to their destination, if possible getting in touch with the Pittsburgh crony when he reached the city.

The pursuer then ate a ham sandwich with liberal washings of liquid fire while he awaited replies to some of his messages; and as soon as he was satisfied that he had set justice in motion he hired an automobile and hied him across country to catch a midnight express to Pittsburgh. He had given orders that his man and accompanying lady should be held in Pittsburgh until his arrival, and he had no doubt but that the orders would be carried out, so sure was he that he was on the right track, and that his cronies would be able and willing to follow his orders.

There was some kind of an excursion on at Pittsburgh, and the place was crowded. The train-men kept calling off specials, and crowds hurried out of the waiting room, only to be replaced by other crowds, all eager, pushing, talking, laughing. They were mostly men, but a good many women and some children seemed to be of the number; and the noise and excitement worried her after her own exciting afternoon. Celia longed to lay her down and sleep, but the seat was narrow, and hard, and people were pressing on every side. That disagreeable man in the slouch hat would stand too near. He was most repulsive looking, though he did not seem to be aware of her presence.

Gordon had a long wait before he finally secured the coveted state-room and started back to her, when suddenly a face that he knew loomed up in the crowd and startled him. It was the face of a private detective who was well known about Washington, but whose headquarters were in New York.

Until that instant, it had not occurred to him to fear watchers so far south and west as Pittsburgh. It was not possible that the other bridegroom would think to track him here, and, as for the Holman contingent, they would not be likely to make a public disturbance about his disappearance, lest they be found to have some connection with the first theft of government property. They could have watchers only through private means, and they must have been wily indeed if they had anticipated his move through Pittsburgh to Washington. Still, it was the natural move for him to make in order to get home as quickly as possible and yet escape them. And this man in the crowd was the very one whom they would have been likely to pick out for their work. He was as slippery in his dealings as they must be, and no doubt was in league with them. He knew the man and his ways thoroughly, and had no mind to fall into his hands.

Whether he had been seen by the detective yet or not, he could not tell, but he suspected he had, by the way the man stood around and avoided recognizing him. There was not an instant to be lost. The fine state-room must go untenanted. He must make a dash for liberty. Liberty! Ah, East Liberty! What queer things these brains of ours are! He knew Pittsburgh just a little. He remembered having caught a train at East Liberty Station once when he had not time to come down to the station to take it. Perhaps he might get the same train at East Liberty. It was nearly two hours before it left.

Swooping down upon the baggage, he murmured in the girl's ear:

"Can you hurry a little? We must catch a car right away."

She followed him closely through the crowd, he stooping as if to look down at his suit-case, so that his height might not attract the attention of the man whose recognition he feared, and in a moment more they were out in the lighted blackness of the streets. One glance backward showed his supposed enemy stretching his neck above the crowd, as if searching for some one, as he walked hurriedly toward the very doorway they had just passed. Behind them shadowed the man in the slouch hat, and with a curious motion of his hand signalled another like himself, the Pittsburgh crony, who skulked in the darkness outside. Instantly this man gave another signal and out of the gloom of the street a carriage drew up at the curb before the door, the cabman looking eagerly for patronage.

Gordon put both suit-cases in one hand and taking Celia's arm as gently as he could in his haste hurried her toward the carriage. It was the very refuge he sought. He placed her inside and gave the order for East Liberty Station, drawing a long breath of relief at being safely out of the station. He did not see the shabby one who mounted the box beside the driver and gave his directions in guttural whispers, nor the man with the slouch hat who watched from the doorway and followed them to a familiar haunt on the nearest car. He only felt how good it was to be by themselves once more where they could talk together without interruption.

But conversation was not easy under the circumstances. The noise of wagons, trains and cars was so great at the station that they could think of nothing but the din, and when they had threaded their way out of the tangle and started rattling over the pavement the driver went at such a furious pace that they could still only converse by shouting and that not at all satisfactorily. It seemed a strange thing that any cabman should drive at such a rapid rate within the city limits, but as Gordon was anxious to get away from the station and the keen-eyed detective as fast as possible he thought nothing of it at first. After a shouted word or two they ceased to try to talk, and Gordon, half shyly, reached out a reassuring hand and laid it on the girl's shrinking one that lay in her lap. He had not meant to keep it there but a second, just to make her understand that all was well, and he would soon be able to explain things, but as she did not seem to resent it nor draw her own away, he yielded to the temptation and kept the small gloved hand in his.

The carriage rattled on, bumpety-bump, over rough places, around corners, tilting now and then sideways, and Celia, half frightened, was forced to cling to her protector to keep from being thrown on the floor of the cab.

"Oh, are we running away?" she breathed awesomely into his ear.

"I think not, — dear," he answered back, the last word inaudible. "The driver thinks we are in a hurry but he has no need to go at this furious pace. I will tell him."

He leaned forward and tapped on the glass, but the driver paid no attention whatever save perhaps to drive faster.

Could it be that he had lost control of his horse and could not stop, or hadn't he heard? Gordon tried again, and accompanied the knocking this time with a shout, but all to no purpose. The cab rattled steadily on. Gordon discovered now that there were two men on the box instead of one and a sudden premonition sent a thrill of alarm through him. What if after all the presence of that detective had been a warning, and he unheeding had walked into a trap? What a fool he had been to get into a carriage where he was at the mercy of the driver. He ought to have stayed in open places where kidnapping would be impossible. Now that he had thought of it he felt convinced that this was just what the enemy would try to do, —kidnap him. The more fruitless he found his efforts to make the driver hear him the more he felt convinced that something was wrong. He tried to open the door next him and found it stuck. He put all his strength forth to turn the catch but it held fast. Then a cold sweat stood out upon him and horror filled his mind. His commission with its large significance to the country was in imminent jeopardy. His own life was in all probability hanging in the balance, but most of all he felt the awful peril of the sweet girl by his side. What terrible experiences might be hers within the next hour if his brain and right arm could not protect her. Instinctively his hand went to the pocket where he had kept his revolver ready since ever he had left Washington. Danger should not find him utterly unprepared.

He realized, too, that it was entirely possible, that his alarms were unfounded; that the driver was really taking them to the East Liberty Station; that the door merely stuck, and he was needlessly anxious. He must keep a steady head and not let his companion see that he was nervous. The first thing was to find out if possible where they really were, but that was a difficult task. The street over which they rattled was utterly dark with the gloom of a smoky city added to the night. There were no street lights except at wide intervals, and the buildings appeared to be blank walls of darkness, probably great warehouses. The way was narrow, and entirely unknown. Gordon could not tell if he had ever been there before. He was sure from his knowledge of the stations that they had gone much farther than to East Liberty, and the darkness and loneliness of the region through which they were passing filled him again with a vague alarm. It occurred to him that he might be able to get the window sash down and speak to the driver, and he struggled with the one on his own side for awhile, with little result, for it seemed to have been plugged up with wads of paper all around. This fact renewed his anxiety. It began to look as if there was intention in sealing up that carriage. He leaned over and felt around the sash of the opposite door and found the paper wads there also. There certainly was intention. Not to alarm Celia he straightened back and went to work again at his own window sash cautiously pulling out the paper until at last he could let down the glass.

A rush of dank air rewarded his efforts, and the girl drew a breath of relief. Gordon never knew how near she had been to fainting at that moment. She was sitting perfectly quiet in her corner watching him, her fears kept to herself, though her heart was beating wildly. She was convinced that the horse was running away.

Gordon leaned his head out of the window, but immediately he caught the gleam of a revolver in a hand that hung at the side of the driver's box, pointed downward straight toward his face as if with intention to be ready in case of need. The owner of the hand was not looking toward him but was talking in muffled tones to the driver. They evidently had not heard the window let down, but were ready for the first sign of an attempt on the part of their victims to escape.

Quietly Gordon drew in his head speculating rapidly on the possibility of wrenching that revolver out of its owner's hand. He could do it from where he sat, but would it be wise? They were probably locked in a trap, and the driver was very likely armed also. What chance would he have to save Celia if he brought on a desperate fight at this point? If he were alone he might knock that revolver out of the man's hand and spring from the window, taking his chance of getting away, but now he had Celia to think of and the case was different. Not for a universe of governments could he leave a woman in such desperate straits. She must be considered first even ahead of the message. This was life and death.

He wondered at his own coolness as he sat back in the carriage and quietly lifted the glass frame back into place. Then he laid a steady hand on Celia's again and stooping close whispered into her ear:

"I am afraid there's something wrong with our driver. Can you be a little brave, — dear?" He did not know he had used the last word this time, but it thrilled into the girl's heart with a sudden accession of trust.

"Oh, yes," she breathed close to his face. "You don't think he has been drinking, do you?"

"Well, perhaps," said Gordon relieved at the explanation. "But keep calm. I think we can get out of this all right. Suppose you change seats with me and let me try if that door will open easily. We might want to get out in a hurry in case he slows up somewhere pretty soon."

Celia quietly and swiftly slipped into Gordon's seat and he applied himself with all his strength and ingenuity gently manipulating the latch and pressing his shoulder against the door, until at last to his joy it gave way reluctantly and he found that it would swing open. He had worked carefully, else the sudden giving of the latch would have thrown him out of the carriage and given instant alarm to his driver. He was so thoroughly convinced by this time that he was being kidnapped, perhaps to be murdered, that every sense was on alert. It was his characteristic to be exceedingly cool during a crisis. It was the quality that the keen-eyed chief had valued most in him, and the final reason why he had been selected for this difficult task in place of an older and more experienced man who at times lost his head.

The door to the outside world being open, Gordon cautiously took a survey of the enemy from that side. There was no gleaming weapon here. The man set grimly enough, laying on the whip and muttering curses to his bony horse who galloped recklessly on as if partaking of the desperate desires of his master. In the distance Gordon would hear the rumbling of an on-coming train. The street was still dark and scarcely a vehicle or person to be seen. There seemed no help at hand, and no opportunity to get out, for they were still rushing at a tremendous pace. An attempt to jump now would very likely result in broken limbs, which would only leave them in a worse plight than they were. He slipped back to his own seat and put Celia next to the free door again. She must be where she could get out first if the opportunity presented itself. Also, he must manage to throw out the suitcases if possible on account of the letters and valuables they contained.

Instinctively his hand sought Celia's in the darkness again, and hers nestled into it in a frightened way as if his strength gave her comfort.

Then, before they could speak or realize, there came the rushing sound of a train almost upon them and the cab came to a halt with a jerk, the driver pulling the horse far back on his haunches to stop him. The shock almost threw Celia to the floor, but Gordon's arm about her steadied her, and instantly he was on the alert.

13

GLANCING through the window he saw that they were in front of a railroad track upon which a long freight train was rushing madly along at a giddy pace for a mere freight. The driver had evidently hoped to pass this point before the train got there, but had failed. The train had an exultant sound as if it knew and had outwitted the driver.

On one side of the street were high buildings and on the other a great lumber yard, between which and their carriage there stood a team of horses hitched to a covered wagon, from the back of which some boards protruded, and this was on the side next to Celia where the door would open! Gordon's heart leaped up with hope and wonder over the miracle of their opportunity. The best thing about their situation was that their driver had stopped just a little back of the covered wagon, so that their door would open to the street directly behind the covered wagon. It made it possible for the carriage door to swing wide and for them to slip across behind the wagon without getting too near to the driver. Nothing could have been better arranged for their escape and the clatter of the empty freight cars drowned all sounds.

Without delay Gordon softly unlatched the door and swung it open whispering to Celia:

"Go! Quick! Over there by the fence in the shadow. Don't look around nor speak! Quick! I'll come!"

Trembling in every limb yet with brave starry eyes Celia slipped like a wraith from the carriage, stole behind the boards and melted into the shadow of the great fence of the lumber yard, and her purple plumes were depths of shadow against the smoky planks. Gordon, grasping the suit-cases moved instantly after her, deftly and silently closing the carriage door and dropping into the shadows behind the big wagon, scarcely able to believe as yet that they had really escaped.

Ten feet back along the sidewalk was a gateway, the post being tall and thick. The gate itself was closed but it hung a few inches inside the line of the fence, and into this depression the two stepped softly and stood, flattening themselves back against the gate as closely as possible, scarcely daring to breathe, while the long freight clattered and rambled it way by like a lot of jolly washerwomen running and laughing in a line and spatting their tired noisy feet as they went then the vehicles impatiently took up their onward course Gordon saw the driver look down at the window below him and glance back hastily over his shoulder, and the man on the other side of the box, looked down on his side. The glitter of something in his hand shone for an instant in the glare of the signal light over the track. Then the horse lurched forward and the cab began its crazy gait over the track and up the cobbled street. They had started onward without getting down to look in the carriage and see if all were safe with their prisoners, and they had not even looked back to see if they had escaped. They evidently trusted in the means the had used to lock the carriage doors, and had heard no sound of their escaping. It was incredible, but it was true. Gordon drew a long breath of relief and relaxed from his strained position. The next thing was to get out of that neighborhood as swiftly as possible before those men had time to discover that their birds had flown. They would of course know at once where their departure had taken place and come back swiftly to search for them, with perhaps more men to help; and a second time escape would be impossible.

Gordon snatched up the suit-cases with one hand, and with the other drew Celia's arm within his.

"Now, we must hurry with all our might," he said softly. "Are you all right?"

"Yes." Her breath was coming in a sob, but her eyes were shining bravely.

"Poor child!" his voice was very tender. "Were you much frightened?"

"A little," she answered more bravely now.

"I shall have hard work to forgive myself for all this," he said tenderly. "But we mustn't talk. We have to get out of this quickly or they may came back after us. Lean on me and walk as fast as you can."

Celia bent her efforts to take long springing strides, and together they fairly skimmed the pavements, turning first this corner, then that, in the general direction from which Gordon thought they had come, until at last, three blocks away they caught the welcome whirr of a trolley, and breathless, flew onward, just catching a car. They cared not where it went so that they were safe in a bright light with other people. No diamonds on any gentleman's neckscarf ever shone to Celia's eyes with so friendly a welcome as the dull brass buttons on that trolley conductor's coat as he rang up their fares and answered Gordon's questions about how to get to East Liberty Station; and their pleasant homely gleam almost were her undoing, for now that they were safe at last the tears would come to her eyes.

Gordon watched her lovingly, tenderly, glad that she did not know how terrible had been her danger. His heart was still beating wildly with the thought of their marvellous escape, and his own present responsibility. He must run no further risks. They would keep to crowded trolleys, and trust to hiding in the open. The main thing was to get out of the city on the first train they could manage to board.

When they reached East Liberty Station a long train was just coming in, all sleepers, and they could hear the echo of a stentorian voice:

"Special for Harrisburg, Baltimore and Washington! All aboard!" and up at the further end of the platform Gordon saw the lank form of the detective whom he had tried to avoid an hour before at the other station.

Without taking time for thought he hurried Celia forward and they sprang breathlessly aboard. Not until they were fairly in the cars and the wheels moving under them did it occur to him that his companion had had nothing to eat since about twelve o'clock. She must be famished, and in a fair way to be ill again. What a fool he was not to have thought! They could have stopped in some obscure restaurant along the way as well as not, and taken a later train, and yet it was safer to get away at once. Without doubt there were watchers at East Liberty, too, and he was lucky to have got on the train without a challenge. He was sure that detective's face lighted strangely as he looked his way. Perhaps there was a buffet attached to the train. At least, he would investigate. If there wasn't, they must get off at the next stop — there must be another stop surely somewhere near the city — he could not remember, but there surely must be.

They had to wait some time to get the attention of the conductor. He was having much trouble with some disgruntled passengers who each claimed to have the same berth. Gordon finally got his ear, and showing his stateroom tickets enquired if they could be used on this train.

"No," growled the worried conductor. "You're on the wrong train. This is a special, and every berth in the train is taken now but one upper."

"Then, we'll have to get off at the next stop, I suppose, and take the other train," said Gordon dismally.

"There isn't any other stop till somewhere in the middle of the night. I tell you this is a special, and we're scheduled to go straight through. East Liberty's the last stop."

"Then what shall we do?" asked Gordon inanely.

"I'm sure I don't know," snapped the conductor. "I've enough to do without mending other people's mistakes. Stay aboard, I suppose, unless you want to jump off and commit suicide."

"But I have a lady with me who isn't at all well," said Gordon, with dignity.

"So much the worse for the lady," replied the conductor inhumanly. "There's one upper berth, I told you."

"An upper berth wouldn't do for her," said Gordon decidedly. "She isn't well, I tell you."

"Suit yourself!" snapped the harassed official. "I reckon it's better than nothing. You may not have it long. I'm likely to be asked for it the next half minute."

"Is that so? And is there absolutely nothing else?"

"Young man, I can't waste words on you. I haven't time. Take it or let it alone. It's all one to me. There's some standing room left in the day-coach, perhaps."

"I'll take it," said Gordon meekly, wishing he could go back and undo the last half-hour. How in the world was he to go and tell Celia that he could provide her nothing better than an upper berth?

She was sitting with her back to him, her face resting wearily on her hand against the window. Two men with largely checked suits, big seal rings, and diamond scarf-pins sat in the opposite seat. He knew it was most unpleasant for her. A nondescript woman with a very large hat and thick powder on her face shared Celia's seat. He reflected that "specials" did not always bear a select company.

"Is there nothing you can do?" he pleaded with the conductor, as he took the bit of pasteboard entitling him to the last vacant berth. "Don't you suppose you could get some man to change and give her a lower berth? It'll be very hard for her. She isn't used to upper berths."

His eyes rested wistfully on the bowed head. Celia had

taken off her plumed hat, and the fitful light of the car played with the gold of her hair. The conductor's grim eye softened as he looked.

"That the lady? I'll see what I can do," he said briefly, and stumped off to the next car. The miracle of her presence worked its change upon him.

Gordon went over to Celia and told her in a low tone that he hoped to have arrangements made for her soon, so that she could be comfortable. She must be fearfully tired with the excitement and fright and hurry. He added that he had made a great blunder in getting on this train, and now there was no chance to get off for several hours, perhaps, and probably no supper to be had.

"Oh, it doesn't matter in the least," said Celia wearily. "I'm not at all hungry." She almost smiled when she said it. He knew that what she wanted was to have her mind relieved about the letters. But she readily saw that there was no opportunity now.

She even seemed sorry at his troubled look, and tried to smile again through the settled sadness in her eyes. He could see she was very weary, and he felt like a great brute in care of a child, and mentally berated himself for his own thoughtlessness.

Gordon started off to search for something to eat for her, and was more successful than he had dared hope. The newsboy had two chicken sandwiches left, and these, with the addition of a fine orange, a box of chocolates, and a glass of ice-water, he presently brought to her, and was rewarded by a smile this time, almost as warm and intimate as those she had given him during their beautiful day.

But he could not sit beside her, for the places were all taken, and he could not stand in the aisle and talk, for the porter was constantly running back and forth making up the berths. There seemed to be a congested state of things in the whole train, every seat being full and men standing in the aisles. He noticed now that they all wore badges of some fraternal order. It was doubtless a delegation to some great convention, upon which they had intruded. They were a good-natured, noisy, happy crowd, but not anywhere among them was to be found a quiet spot where he and Celia could go on with their suddenly interrupted conversation. Presently the conductor came to him and said he had found a gentleman who would give the lady his lower berth and take her upper one. It was already made up, and the lady might take possession at once.

Gordon made the exchange of tickets, and immediately escorted Celia to it. He found her most glad to go for she was now unutterably weary, and was longing to get away from the light and noise about her.

He led the way with the suit-cases, hoping that in the other car there would be some spot where they could talk for a few minutes. But he was disappointed. It was even fuller than in the first car. He arranged everything for her comfort as far as possible, disposed of her hat and fixed her suit-case so that she could open it, but even while he was doing it there were people crowding by, and no private conversation could be had. He stepped back when all was arranged and held the curtain aside that she might sit on the edge of her berth. Then stooping over he whispered:

"Try to trust me until morning. I'll explain it all to you then, so that you will understand how I have had nothing to do with those letters. Forget it, and try to rest. Will you?"

His tone was wistful. He had never wanted to do anything so much in all his life as to stoop and kiss those sweet lips, and the lovely eyes that looked up at him out of the dusky shadows of the berth, filled with fear and longing. They looked more than ever like the blue tired flowers that drooped from her gown wearily. But he held himself with a firm hand. She was not his to kiss. When she knew how he had deceived her, she would probably never give him the right to kiss her.

"I will try," she murmured in answer to his question, and

then added: "But where will you be? Is your berth near by?"

"Not far away—that is, I had to take a place in another car, they are so crowded."

"Oh!" she said a little anxiously. "Are you sure you have a good comfortable place?"

"Oh, yes, I shall be all right," he answered joyously. It was so wonderful to have her care whether he was comfortable or not.

The porter was making up the opposite berth, and there was no room to stand longer, so he bade her good night, she putting out her hand for a farewell. For an instant he held it close, with gentle pressure, as if to reassure her, then he went away to the day-coach, and settled down into a hard corner at the very back of the car, drawing his travelling cap over his eyes, and letting his heart beat out wild joy over that little touch of her dear hand. Wave after wave of sweetness went over him, thrilling his very soul with a joy he had never known before.

And this was love! And what kind of a wretch was he, presuming to love like this a woman who was the promised bride of another man! Ah, but such a man! A villain! A brute, who had used his power over her to make her suffer tortures! Had a man like that a right to claim her? His whole being answered "no."

Then the memory of the look in her eyes, the turn of her head, the soft touch of her fingers as they lay for that instant in his, the inflection of her voice, would send that wave of sweetness over his senses, his heart would thrill anew, and he would forget the wretch who stood between him and this lovely girl whom he knew now he loved as he had never dreamed a man could love.

Gradually his mind steadied itself under the sweet intoxication, and he began to wonder just what he should say to her in the morning. It was a good thing he had not had further opportunity to talk with her that night, for he could not have told her everything; and now if all went well they would be in Washington in the morning, and he might make some excuse till after he had delivered his message. Then he would be free to tell the whole story, and lay his case before her for decision. His heart throbbed with ecstasy as he thought of the possibility of her forgiving him, and yet it seemed most unlikely. Sometimes he would let his wild longings fancy for just an instant what joy it would be if she could be induced to let the marriage stand. But he told himself at the same time that that could never be. It was very likely that there was someone else in New York to whom her heart would turn if she were free from the scoundrel who had threatened her into a compulsory marriage. He would promise to help her, protect her, defend her from the man who was evidently using blackmail to get her into his power for some purpose; most likely for the sake of having control of her property. At least it would be some comfort to be able to help her out of her trouble. And yet, would she ever trust a man who had even unwittingly allowed her to be bound by the sacred tie of marriage to an utter stranger?

And thus, amid hope and fear, the night whirled itself away. Forward in the sleeper the girl lay wide awake for a long time. In the middle of the night a thought suddenly evolved itself out of the blackness of her curtained couch. She sat upright alertly and stared into the darkness, as if it were a thing that she could catch and handle and examine. The thought was born out of a dreamy vision of the crisp brown waves, almost curls if they had not been short and thick, that covered the head of the man who had lain sleeping outside her curtains in the early morning. It came to her with sudden force that not so had been the hair of the boy George Hayne, who used to trouble her girlish days. His was thin and black and oily, collecting naturally into little isolated strings with the least warmth, and giving him the appearance of a kitten who had been out in the rain. One lock, how well she remembered that lock! — one lock on the very crown of his head had always refused to lie down, no matter

how much persuasion was brought to bear upon it. It had
been the one point on which the self-satisfied George had
been pregnable, his hair, that scalp lock that would always
arise stiffly, oilily, from the top of his head. The hair she had
looked at admiringly that morning in the dawning crimson
of the rising sun had not been that way. It had curved cling-
ingly to the shape of the fine head as if it loved to go that
way. It was beautiful and fine and burnished with a sense of
life and vigor in its every wave. Could hair change in ten
years? Could it grow brown where it had been black? Could
it become glossy instead of dull and oily? Could it take on
the signs of natural wave where it had been as straight as a
die? Could it grow like fur where it had been so thin?

The girl could not solve the problem, but the thought was
most startling and brought with it many suggestive possibilities that were most disturbing. Yet gradually out of the
darkness she drew a sort of comfort in her dawning enlight-
enment. Two things she had to go on in her strange premises:
he had said he did not write the letters, and his hair was not
the same. Who then was he? Her husband now undoubtedly,
but who? And if deeds and hair change so materially, why
not spirits? At least he was not the same as she had feared and
dreaded. There was so much comfort.

And at last she lay down and slept.

14

THEY were late coming into Washington, for the Special had been sidetracked in the night for several express trains, and the noisy crowd who had kept one another awake till after midnight made up by sleeping far into the morning.

Three times did Gordon make the journey three cars front to see if his companion of yesterday were awake and needed anything, but each time found the curtains drawn and still, and each time he went slowly back again to his seat in the crowded daycoach.

It was not until the white dome of the capitol, and the tall needle of the monument, were painted soft and vision-like against the sky, reminding one of the pictures of the heavenly city in the story of Pilgrim's Progress, and faintly suggesting a new and visionary world, that he sought her again, and found her fully ready, standing in the aisle while the porter put up the berth out of the way. Beneath the great brim of her purple hat, where the soft fronds of her plumes trembled with the motion of the train, she lifted sweet eyes to him, as if she were both glad and frightened to see him. And then that ecstasy shot through him again, as he realized suddenly what it would be to have her for his life-companion, to feel her looks of gladness were all for him, and have the right to take all fright away from her.

They could only smile at each other for good-morning, for everybody was standing up and being brushed, and pushing here and there for suit-cases and lost umbrellas; and everybody talked loudly, and laughed a great deal, and told how late the train was. Then at last they were there, and could get out and walk silently side by side in the noisy procession through the station to the sidewalk.

What little things sometimes change a lifetime and make for our safety or our destruction! That very morning three keen watchers were set to guard that station at Washington to hunt out the government spy who had stolen back the stolen message, and take him, message and all, dead or alive, back to New York; for the man who could testify against the Holman Combination was not to be let live if there was such a thing as getting him out of the way. But they never thought to watch the Special which was supposed to carry only delegates to the great convention. He could not possibly be on that! They knew he was coming from Pittsburgh, for they had been so advised by telegram the evening before by one of their company who had seen him buying a sleeper ticket for Washington, but they felt safe about that Special, for they had made inquiries and been told no one but delegates could possibly come on it. They had done their work thoroughly, and were on hand with every possible plan perfected for bagging their game, but they took the time when the Pittsburgh Special was expected to arrive for eating a hearty breakfast in the restaurant across the street from the station. Two of them emerged from the restaurant doorway in plenty of time to meet the next Pittsburgh tain, just as Gordon, having placed the lady in a closed carriage, was getting in himself.

If the carriage had stood in any other spot along the pavement in front of the station, they never would have seen him, but, as it was, they had a full view of him; and because they were Washington men, and experts in their line, they recognized him at once, and knew their plans had failed, and that only by extreme measures could they hope to prevent the delivery of the message which would mean downfall and disaster to them and their schemes.

As Gordon slammed shut the door of the carriage, he caught a vision of his two enemies pointing excitedly toward him, and he knew that the blood-hounds were on the scent.

His heart beat wildly. His anxiety was divided between the message and the lady. What should he do? Drive at once to the home of his chief and deliver the message, or leave the girl at his rooms, 'phone for a faster conveyance and trust to getting to his chief ahead of his pursuers?

"Don't let anything hinder you! Don't let anything hinder you! Make it a matter of life and death!" rang the little ditty in his ears, and now it seemed as if he must go straight ahead with the message. And yet—"a matter of life and death!" He could not, must not, might not, take the lady with him into danger. If he must be in danger of death he did not want to die having exposed an innocent stranger to the same.

Then there was another point to be thought of.

He had already told the driver to take him to his apartments, and to drive as rapidly as possible. It would not do to stop him now and change the directions, for a pistol-shot could easily reach him yet; and, coming from a crowd, who would be suspected? His enemies were standing on the threshold of a place where there were many of their kind to protect them, and none of his friends knew of his coming. It would be a race for life from now on to the finish.

Celia was looking out with interest at the streets, recognizing landmarks with wonder, and did not notice Gordon's white, set face and burning eyes as he strained his vision to note how fast the horse was going. Oh, if the driver would only turn off at the next corner into the side street they could not watch the carriage so far, but it was not likely, for this was the most direct road, and yet—yes, he had turned! Joy! The street here was so crowded that he had sought the narrower, less crowded way that he might go the faster.

It seemed an age to him before they stopped at his apartments. To Celia, it had been but a short ride, in which familiar scenes had brought her pleasure, for she recognized that she was not in strange Chicago, but in Washington, a city often visited. Somehow she felt it was an omen of a better future than she had feared.

"Oh, why didn't you tell me?" she smiled to Gordon. "It is Washington, dear old Washington."

Somehow he controlled the tumult in his heart and smiled back, saying in a voice quite natural:

"I am so glad you like it."

She seemed to understand that they could not talk until they reached a quiet place somewhere, and she did not trouble him with questions. Instead—she looked from the window, or watched him furtively, comparing him with her memory of George Hayne, and wondering in her own thoughts. She was glad to have them to herself for just this little bit, for now that the morning had come she was almost afraid of revelation, what it might bring forth. And so it came about that they took the swift ride in more or less silence, and neither thought it strange.

As the carriage stopped, he spoke with low, hurried voice, tense with excitement, but her own nerves were on a strain also, and she did not notice.

"We get out here."

He had the fare ready for the driver, and, stepping out, hurried Celia into the shelter of the hallway. It happened that an elevator had just come down, so it was but a second more before they were up safe in the hall before his own apartment.

Taking a latch-key from his pocket, he applied it to the door, flung it open, and ushered Celia to a large leather chair in the middle of the room. Then, stepping quickly to the side of the room, he touched a bell, and from it went to the telephone, with an "Excuse me, please, this is necessary," to the girl, who sat astonished, wondering at the homelikeness of the room and at the "at-homeness" of the man. She had expected to be taken to a hotel. This seemed to be a private apartment with which he was perfectly acquainted. Perhaps it belonged to some friend. But how, after an absence of years, could he remember just where to go, which door and which elevator to take, and how to fit the key with so accustomed a hand? Then her attention was arrested by his voice:

"Give me 254 L please," he said. . . . "Is this 254 L? . . . Is Mr. Osborne in? . . . You say he has *not* gone to the office yet? . . . May I speak with him? . . . Is this Mr. Osborne? . . . I did not expect you to know my voice. . . . Yes, sir; just arrived, and all safe so far. Shall I bring it to the house or the office? . . . The house? . . . All right, sir. Immediately. . . . By the way, I am sure Hal and Burke are on my track. They saw me at the station. . . . To your house? . . . You will wait until I come? . . . All right, sir. Yes, immediately. . . . Sure, I'll take precaution. . . . Good-by."

With the closing words came a tap at the door.

"Come, Henry," he answered, as the astonished girl turned toward the door. "Henry, you will go down, please, to the restaurant, and bring up a menu card. This lady will select what she would like to have, and you will serve breakfast for her in this room as soon as possible. I shall be out for perhaps an hour, and, meantime, you will obey any orders she may give you."

He did not introduce her as his wife, but she did not notice the omission. She had suddenly become aware of a strange, distraught haste in his manner, and when he said he was going out alarm seized her, she could not tell why.

The man bowed deferentially to his master, looked his admiration and devotion to the lady, waited long enough to say:

"I'se mighty glad to see you safe back, sah—" and disappeared to obey orders.

Celia turned toward Gordon for an explanation, but he was already at the telephone again:

"46! . . . Is this the Garage? . . . This is The Harris Apartments. . . . Can you send Thomas with a closed car to the rear door immediately? . . . Yes. . . . No, I want Thomas, and a car that can speed. . . . Yes, the rear door, *rear,* and at once. . . . What? . . . What's that? . . . But I *must.* . . . It's *official* business. . . . Well, I thought so. Hurry them up. Good-by."

He turned and saw her troubled gaze following him with growing fear in her eyes.

"What is the matter?" she asked anxiously. "Has something happened?"

Just one moment he paused, and, coming toward her, laid his hands of hers tenderly.

"Nothing the matter at all," he said soothingly. "At least nothing that need worry you. It is just a matter of pressing business. I'm sorry to have to go from you for a little while, but it's necessary. I cannot explain to you until I return. You will trust me? You will not worry?"

"I will try!"

Her lips were quivering, and her eyes were filled with tears. Again he felt that intense longing to lay his lips upon hers and comfort her, but he put it from him.

"There is nothing to feel sad about," he said, smiling gently. "It is nothing tragic only there is need for haste, for if I wait, I may fail yet—It is something that means a great deal to me. When I come back I will explain all."

"Go!" she said, putting out her hands in a gesture of resignation, as if she would hurry him from her. And though she was burning to know what it all meant there was that about him that compelled her to trust him and to wait.

Then his control almost went from him. He nearly took those hands in his and kissed them, but he did not. Instead, he went with swift steps to his bedroom door, threw open a chiffonier drawer, and took therefrom something small and sinister. She could see the gleam of its polished metal, and she sensed a strange little menace in the click as he did something to it. He came out with his hand in his pocket, as if he had just hidden something there.

She was not familiar with firearms. Her mother had been afraid of them and her brother had never flourished any around the house, yet she knew by instinct that some weapon of defence was in Gordon's possession; and a nameless horror rose in her heart and shone from her blue eyes, but she would not speak a word to let him know it. If he had not been in such haste, he would have seen. Her horror would have been still greater if she had known that he already carried one loaded revolver and was taking a second in case of an emergency.

"Don't worry," he called as he hurried out the door. "Henry will get anything you need, and I shall soon be back."

The door closed and he was gone. She heard his quick step down the hall, heard the elevator door slide and slam again, and then she knew he was gone down. Outside an automobile sounded and she seemed to hear again his words at the phone, "The rear door." Why had he gone to the rear door? Was he in hiding? Was he flying from someone? What, oh what, did it mean?

Without stopping to reason it out, she flew across the room and opened the door of the bedroom he had just left, then through it passed swiftly to a bathroom beyond. Yes, there was a window. Would it be the one? Could she see him? And what good would it do her if she could?

She crowded close to the window. There was a heavy sash with stained glass, but she selected a clear bit of yellow and put her eye close. Yes, there was a closed automobile just below her, and it had started away from the building. He had gone, then. Where?

Her mind was a blank for a few minutes. She went slowly, mechanically back to the other room without noticing anything about her, sat down in the chair, putting her hands to her temples, and tried to think. Back to the moment in the church where he had appeared at her side and the service had begun. Something had told her then that he was different, and yet there had been those letters, and how could it possibly be that he had not written them? He was gone on some dangerous business. Of that she felt sure. There had been some caution given him by the man to whom he first 'phoned. He had promised to take precaution — that meant the little, wicked, gleaming thing in his pocket. Perhaps some harm would come to him, and she would never know. And then she stared at the opposite wall with wonder-filled eyes. Well, and suppose it did? Why did she care? Was he not the man whose power over her but two short days ago would have made her welcome death as her deliverer? Why was all changed now? Just because he had smiled upon her and been kind? Had given her a few wild flowers and said her eyes were like them? Had hair that waved instead of being straight and thin? And where was all her loyalty to her dear dead father's memory? How could she mind that danger should come to one who had threatened to tell terrible lies that should blacken him in the thoughts of people who had loved him? Had she forgotten the letters? Was she willing to forgive all just because he had declared that he did not write them? How foolish! He said he could prove that he did not, but of course that was all nonsense. He must have written them. And yet there was the wave in his hair, and the kindness in his eyes. And he had looked — oh, he had looked terrible things when he had read that letter; as if he would like to wreak vengeance on the man who had written it. Could a man masquerade that way?

And then a new solution to the problem came to her. Suppose this — whoever he was — this man who had married her, had gone out to find and punish George Hayne? Suppose — But then she covered her eyes with her hands and shuttered. Yet why should she care? But she did. Suppose he should be killed, himself! Who was he if not George Hayne and how did he come to take his place? Was it just another of George's terrible tricks upon her?

A quick vision came of their bringing him back to her. He would lie, perhaps, on that great crimson leather couch over there, just as he had lain in the dawning of the morning in the state-room of the train, with his hands hanging limp, and one perhaps across his breast, as if he were guarding something, and his bright waves of brown hair lying heavy about his forehead — only, his forehead would be white, so white and cold, with a little blue mark in his temple perhaps.

The footsteps of the man Henry brought her back to the present again. She smiled at him pleasantly as he entered, and answered his questions about what she would have for breakfast; but it was he who selected the menu, not she, and after he had gone she could not have told what she had ordered. She could not get away from the vision on the couch. She closed her eyes and pressed her cold fingers against her eyeballs to drive it away, but still her bridegroom seemed to lie there before her.

The colored man came back presently with a loaded tray, and set it down on a little table which he wheeled before her, as though he had done it many times before. She thanked him, and said there was nothing else she needed, so he went away.

She toyed with the cup of delicious coffee which he had poured for her, and the few swallows she took gave her new heart. She broke a bit from a hot roll, and ate a little of the delicious steak, but still her mind was at work at the problem, and her heart was full of nameless anxiety.

He had gone away without any breakfast himself, and he had had no supper the night before, she was sure. He probably had given to her everything he could get on the train. She was haunted with regret because she had not shared with him. She got up and walked about the room, trying to shake off the horror that was upon her, and the dread of what the morning might bring forth. Ordinarily she would have thought of sending a message to her mother and brother, but her mind was so troubled now that it never occurred to her.

The walls of the room were tinted a soft greenish gray, and above the picture moulding they blended into a woodsy landscape with a hint of water, greensward, and blue sky through interlacing branches. It reminded her of the little village they had seen as they started from the train in the early morning light. What a beautiful day they had spent together and how it had changed her whole attitude of heart toward the man she had married!

Two or three fine pictures were hung in good lights. She studied them, and knew that the one who had selected and hung them was a judge of true art; but they did not hold her attention long, for as yet, she had not connected the room with the man for whom she waited.

A handsome mahogany desk stood open in a broad space by the window. She was attracted by a little painted miniature of a woman. She took it up and studied the face. It was fine and sweet, with brown hair dressed low, and eyes that reminded her of the man who had just gone from her. Was this, then, the home of some relative with whom he had come to stop for a day or two, and, if so, where was the relative? The dress in the miniature was of a quarter of a century past, yet the face was young and sweet, as young, perhaps, as herself. She wondered who it was. She put the miniature back in place with caressing hand. She felt that she would like to know this woman with the tender eyes. She wished her here now, that she might tell her all her anxiety.

Her eye wandered to the pile of letters, some of them official-looking ones, one or two in square, perfumed envelopes, with high, angular writing. They were all addressed to Mr. Cyril Gordon. That was strange! Who was Mr. Cyril Gordon? What had they—what had she—to do with him? Was he a friend whom George—whom they—were visiting for a few days? It was all bewildering.

Then the telephone rang.

Her heart beat wildly and she looked toward it as if it had been a human voice speaking and she had no power to answer. What should she do now? Should she answer? Or should she wait for the man to come? Could the man hear the telephone bell or was she perhaps expected to answer? And yet if Mr. Cyril Gordon—well, somebody ought to answer. The 'phone rang insistently once more, and still a third time. What if *he* should be calling her? Perhaps he was in distress. This thought sent her flying to the 'phone. She took down the receiver and called:

"Hello!" and her voice sounded far away to herself.

"Is this Mr. Gordon's apartment?"

"Yes," she answered, for her eyes were resting on the pile of letters close at hand.

"Is Mr. Gordon there?"

"No he is not," she answered, growing more confident now and almost wishing she had not presumed to answer a stranger's 'phone.

"Why, I just 'phoned to the office and they told me he had returned," said a voice that had an imperious note in it. "Are you sure he isn't there?"

"Quite sure," she replied.

"Who is this, please?"

"I beg your pardon," said Celia trying to make time and knowing not how to reply. She was not any longer Miss Hathaway. Who was she? Mrs. Hayne? She shrank from the name. It was filled with horror for her. "Who is this, I said," snapped the other voice now. "Is this the chambermaid? Because if it is I'd like you to look around and inquire and be quite sure that Mr. Gordon isn't there. I wish to speak with him about something very important."

Celia smiled.

"No, this is not the chambermaid," she said sweetly, "and I am quite sure Mr. Gordon is not here."

"How long before he will be there?"

"I don't know really, for I have just come myself."

"Who is this to whom I am talking?"

"Why—just a friend," she answered, wondering if that were the best thing to say.

"Oh!" there was a long and contemplative pause at the other end.

"Well, could you give Mr. Gordon a message when he comes in?"

"Why certainly, I think so. Who is this?'"

"Miss Bentley. Julia Bentley. He'll know," replied the imperious one eagerly now. "And tell him please that he is expected here to dinner to-night. We need him to complete the number, and he simply mustn't fail me. I'll excuse him for going off in such a rush if he comes early and tells me all about it. Now you won't forget, will you? You got the name, Bentley, did you? B, E, N, T, L, E, Y, you know. And you'll tell him the minute he comes in?"

"Yes."

"Thank you! What did you say your name was?"

But Celia had hung up. Somehow the message annoyed her, she could not tell why. She wished she had not answered the 'phone. Whoever Mr. Cyril Gordon was what should she do if he should suddenly appear? And as for this imperious lady and her message she hoped she would never have to deliver it. On second thought why not write it and leave it on his desk with the pile of letters? She would do it. It would serve to pass away a few of these dreadful minutes that lagged so distressfully.

She sat down and wrote: "Miss Bentley wishes Mr. Gordon to dine with her this evening. She will pardon his running away the other day if he will come early." She laid it beside the high angular writing on the square perfumed letters and went back to the leather chair too restless to rest yet too weary to stand up.

She went presently to the back windows to look out and then to the side ones. Across the housetops she could catch a glimpse of domes and buildings. There was the Congressional Library, which usually delighted her with its exquisite tones of gold and brown and white. But she had no eyes for it now. Beyond were more buildings, all set in the lovely foliage which was much farther developed than it had been in New York State. From another window she could get a glimpse of the Potomac shining in the morning sun.

She wandered to the front windows and looked out. There were people passing and repassing. It was a busy street, but she could not make out whether it was one she knew or not. There were two men walking back and forth on the opposite side. They did not go further than the corner of the street either way. They looked across at the windows sometimes and pointed up, when they met, and once one of them took something out of his pocket and flashed it under his coat at his side, as if to have it ready for use. It reminded her of the thing her husband had held in his hand in the bedroom and she shuddered. She watched them, fascinated, not able to draw herself away from the window.

Now and then she would go to the rear window, to see if there was any sign of the automobile returning, and then hurry back to the front, to see if the men were still there. Once she returned to the chair, and, lying back, shut her eyes, and let the memory of yesterday sweep over her in all its sweet details, up to the time when they had got into the way train and she had seemed to feel her disloyalty to her father. But now her heart was all on the other side, and she began to feel that there had been some dreadful mistake, somewhere, and he was surely all right. He could not, could not have written those terrible letters. Then again the details of their wild carriage ride in Pittsburgh and miraculous escape haunted her. There was something strange and unexplained about that which she must understand.

15

MEANTIME, Gordon was speeding away to another part of the city by the fastest time an experienced chauffeur dare to make. About the time they turned the first corner into the avenue, two burly policemen sauntered casually into the pretty square in front of the house where lived the chief of the Secret Service. There was nothing about their demeanor to show that they had been detailed there by special urgency, and three men who hurried to the little park just across the street from the house could not possibly know that their leisurely and careless stroll was the result of a hurried telephone message from the chief to police headquarters immediately after his message from Gordon.

The policemen strolled by the house, greeted each other, and walked on around the square across the little park. They eyed the three men sitting idly on a bench, and passed leisurely on. They disappeared around a corner, and to the three men were out of the way. The latter did not know the hidden places where the officers took up their watch, and when an automobile appeared, and the three stealthily got up from their park bench and distributed themselves among the shrubbery near the walk, they knew not that their every movement was observed with keen attention. But they did wonder how it happened that those two policemen seemed to spring out of the ground suddenly, just as the auto came to a halt in front of the chief's house.

Gordon sprang out and up the steps with a bound, the door opening before him as if he were expected. The two grim and apparently indifferent policemen stood outside like two stone images on guard, while up the street with the rhythmic sound rode two mounted police, also coming to a halt before the house as if for a purpose. The three men in the bushes hid their instruments of death, and would have slunk away had there been a chance; but, turning to make a hasty flight, they were met by three more policemen. There was the crack of a revolver as one of the three desperadoes tried a last reckless dash for freedom—and failed. The wretch went to justice with his right arm hanging limp by his side.

Inside the house Gordon was delivering up his message, and as he laid it before his chief, and stood silent while the elder man read and pondered its tremendous import, it occurred to him for the first time that his chief would require some report of his journey, and the hindrances that had made him a whole day late in getting back to Washington. His heart stood still with sudden panic. What was he to do? How could he tell it all? What right had he to tell of his marriage to an unknown woman? A marriage that perhaps was not a marriage. He could not know what the outcome would be until he had told the girl everything. As far as he himself was concerned he knew that the great joy of his life had come to him in her. And he must think of her and protect her good name in every way. If there should be such a thing as that she should consent to remain with him and be his wife he must never let a soul know but what the marriage had been planned long ago. It would not be fair to her. It would make life intolerable for them both either together or apart. And while he might be and doubtless was perfectly safe in confiding in his chief, and asking him to keep silence about the matter, still he felt that even that would be a breach of faith with Celia. He must close his lips upon the story until he could talk with her and know her wishes. He drew a sigh of weariness. It was a long, hard way he had come, and it was not over. The worst ordeal would be his confession to the bride who was not his wife.

The chief looked up.

"Could you make this out, Gordon?" he asked, noting keenly the young man's weary eyes, the strained, tense look about his mouth.

"Oh, yes sir; I saw it at once. I was almost afraid my eyes might betray the secret before I got away with it."

"Then you know that you have saved the country, and what you have been worth to the Service."

The young man flushed with pleasure.

"Thank you, sir," he said, looking down. "I understood it was important, and I am glad I was able to accomplish the errand without failing."

"Have you reason to suppose you were followed, except for what you saw at the station in this city?"

"Yes, sir; I am sure there were detectives after me as I was leaving New York. They were suspicious of me. I saw one of the men who had been at the dinner with me watching me. The disguise — and — some circumstances — threw him off. He wasn't sure. Then, there was a man — you know him, Balder — at Pittsburgh? — "

"Pittsburgh!"

"Yes, you wonder how I got to Pittsburgh. You see, I was shadowed almost from the first I suspect, for when I reached the station in New York I was sure I recognized this man who had sat opposite me a few minutes before. I suppose my disguise, which you so thoughtfully provided, bothered him, for though he followed me about at a little distance he didn't speak to me. I had to get on the first train that circumstances permitted, and perhaps the fact that it was a Chicago train made him think he was mistaken in me. Anyhow I saw no more of him after the train left the station. Rather unexpectedly I found I could get the drawing room compartment, and went into immediate retirement, leaving the train at daylight where it was delayed on a side track, and walked across country till I found a conveyance that took me to Pittsburgh train. It didn't seem feasible to get away from the Chicago train any sooner as the train made no further stops, and it was rather late at night by the time I boarded it. I thought I would run less risk by making a detour. I never dreamed they would have watchers out for me at Pittsburgh, and I can't think yet how they managed to get on my track, but almost the first minute I landed I spied Balder stretching his neck over the crowds. I bolted from the station at once and finding a carriage drawn up before the door just ready for me I got in and ordered them to drive me to East Liberty Station.

"I am afraid I shall always be suspicious of handy closed carriages after this experience. I certainly have reason to be. The door was no sooner closed on me than the driver began to race like mad through the streets. I didn't think much of it at first until he had been going some time, fully long enough to have reached East Liberty, and the horse was still rushing like a locomotive. Then I saw that we were in a lonely district of the city that seemed unfamiliar. That alarmed me and I tapped on the window and called to the driver. He paid no attention. Then I found the doors were fastened shut, and the windows plugged so they wouldn't open.

"I discovered that an armed man rode beside the driver. I managed to get one of the doors open after a good deal of work, and escaped when we stopped for a freight train to pass; but I'm satisfied that I was being kidnapped and if I hadn't got away just when I did you would never have heard of me again or the message either. I finally managed to reach East Liberty Station and jumped on the first train that came in, but I caught a glimpse of Balder stretching his neck over the crowd. He must have seen me and had Hale and Burke on the watch when I got here. They just missed me by a half second. They went over to the restaurant—didn't expect me on a special, but I escaped them, and I'm mighty glad to get that little paper into your possession and out of mine. It's rather a long story to tell the whole, but I think you have the main facts."

There was a suspicious glitter in the keen eyes of the kind old chief as he put out his hand and grasped Gordon's in a hearty shake; but all he said was:

"And you are all worn out—I'll guarantee you didn't sleep much last night."

"Well, no," said Gordon; "I had to sit up in a day-coach and share the seat with another man. Besides, I was somewhat excited."

"Of course, of course!" puffed the old chief, coughing vigorously, and showing by his gruff attitude that he was deeply affected. "Well, young man, this won't be forgotten by the Department. Now you go home and take a good sleep. Take the whole day off if you wish, and then come down tomorrow morning and tell me all about it. Isn't there anything more I need to know at once that justice may be done?"

"I believe not," said Gordon, with a sigh of relief. "There's a list of the men who were at dinner with me. I wrote them down from memory last night when I couldn't sleep. I also wrote a few scraps of conversation, which will show you just how deep the plot had gone. If I had not read the message and known its import, I should not have understood what they were talking about."

"H-m! Yes. If there had been more time before you started I might have told you all about it. Still it seemed desirable that you should appear as much at your ease as possible. I thought this would be best accomplished by your knowing nothing of the import of the writing when you first met the people."

"I suppose it was as well that I did not know any more than I did. You are a great chief, sir! I was deeply impressed anew with that fact as I saw how wonderfully you had planned for every possible emergency. It was simply great, sir."

"Pooh! Pooh! Get you home and to bed," said the old chief quite brusquely.

He touched a bell and a man appeared.

"Jessup, is the coast clear?" he asked.

"Yessah," declared the darky. "Dey have jest hed a couple o' shots in de pahk, an' now dey tuk de villains off to der p'lice station. De officers is out der waitin' to 'scort de gemman."

"Get home with you, Gordon, and don't come to the office till ten in the morning. Then come straight to my private room."

Gordon thanked him, and left the room preceded by the gray-haired servant. He was surprised to find the policemen outside, and wondered still more that they seemed to be going one in front and the other behind him as he rode along. He was greatly relieved that he had not been called upon to give the whole story. His heart was filled with anxiety now to get back to the girl, and tell her everything, and yet he dreaded it more than anything he had ever had to face in all his life. He sat back on cushions, and, covering his face with his hands, tried to think how he should begin, but he could see nothing but her sweet eyes filled with tears, think of nothing but the way she had looked and smiled during the beautiful morning they had spent together in the little town of Milton. Beautiful little Milton. Should he ever see it again?

Celia at her window grew more and more nervous as an hour and then another half hour slipped slowly away, and still he did not come. Then two mounted policemen rode rapidly down the street following an automobile, in which sat the man for whom she waited.

She had no eyes now for the men who had been lurking across the way, and when she thought to look for them again she saw them running in the opposite direction as fast as they could go, making wild gestures for a car to stop for them.

She stood by the window and saw Gordon get out of the car, and disappear into the building below, saw the car wheel and curve away and the mounted police take up their stand on either corner; heard the clang of the elevator as it started up, and the clash of its door as it stopped at that floor; heard steps coming on toward the door, and the key in the latch. Then she turned and looked at him, her two hands clasped before her, and her two eyes yearning, glad and fearful all at once.

"Oh, I have been so frightened about you! I am so glad you have come!" she said, and caught her voice in a sob as she took one little step toward him.

He threw his hat upon the floor, wherever it might land, and went to meet her, a great light glowing in his tired eyes, his arms outstretched to hers.

"And did you care?" he asked in a voice of almost awe. "Dear, did you *care* what became of *me?*"

"Oh yes, I *cared!* I could not help it." There was a real sob in her voice now, though her eyes were shining.

His arms went around her hungrily, as if he would draw her to him in spite of everything; yet he kept them so encircling, without touching her, like a benediction that would enwrap the very soul of his beloved. Looking down into her face he breathed softly:

"Oh, my dear, it seems as if I must hold you close and kiss you!"

She looked up with bated breath, and thought she understood. Then, with a lovely gesture of surrender, she whispered, "I can trust you." Her lashes were drooping now over her eyes.

"Not until you know all," he said, and put her gently from him into the great arm-chair, with a look of reverence and self-abnegation she felt she never would forget.

"Then, tell me quickly," she said, a swift fear making her weak from head to foot. She laid her hand across her heart, as if to help steady its beating.

He wheeled forward the leather couch opposite her chair, and sat down, her head drooping, his eyes down. He dreaded to begin.

She waited for the revelation, her eyes upon his bowed head.

Finally he lifted his eyes and saw her look, and a tender light came into his face.

"It is a strange story," he said. "I don't know what you will think of me after it is told, but I want you to know that, blundering, stupid, even criminal, though you may think me, I would sooner die this minute than cause you one more breath of suffering."

Her eyes lit up with a wonderful light, and the ready tears sprang into them, tears that sparkled through the sunshine of a great joy that illumined her whole face.

"Please go on," she said softly, and added very gently, "I believe you."

But even with those words in his ears the beginning was not easy. Gordon drew a deep breath and launched forth.

"I am not the man you think," he said, and looked at her to see how she would take it. "My name is not George Hayne. My name is Cyril Gordon."

As one might launch an arrow at a beloved victim and long that it may not strike the mark, so he sent his truth home to her understanding, and waited in breathless silence, hoping against hope that this might not turn her against him.

"Oh!" she breathed softly, as if some puzzle were solving itself. "Oh! — "this time not altogether in surprise, nor as if the fact were displeasing. She looked at him expectantly for further revelation, and he plunged into his story headlong.

"I'm a member of the Secret Service, — headquarters here in Washington, — and day before yesterday I was sent to New

York on an important errand. A message of great import written in a private code had been stolen from one of our men. I was sent to get it before they could decipher it. The message involved matters of such tremendous significance that I was ordered to go under an assumed name, and on no account to let anyone know of my mission. My orders were to get the message, and let nothing hinder me in bringing it with all haste to Washington. I went with the full understanding that I might even be called upon to risk my life."

He looked up. The girl sat wide-eyed, with hands clasped together at her throat.

He hurried on, not to cause her any needless anxiety.

"I won't weary you with details. There were a good many annoying hindrances on the way, which served to make me nervous, but I carried out the program laid down by my chief, and succeeded in getting possession of the message and making my escape from the house of the man who had stolen it. As I closed the door behind me, knowing that it could be but a matter of a few seconds at longest before six furious men would be on my track, who would stop at nothing to get back what I had taken from them, I saw a carriage standing almost before the house. The driver took me for the man he awaited, and I lost no time in taking advantage of his mistake. I jumped in, telling him to drive as fast as he could. I intended to give him further directions, but he had evidently had them from another quarter, and I thought I could call to him as soon as we were out of the dangerous neighborhood. To add to my situation I soon became sure that an automobile and a motor-cycle were following me. I recognized one of the men in the car as the man who sat opposite to me at the table a few minutes before. My coachman drove like mad, while I hurried to secure the message so that if I were caught it would not be found, and to put on a slight disguise—some eyebrows and things the chief had given me. Before I knew where I was, the carriage had stopped before a building. At first I thought it was a prison—and the car and motor-cycle came to a halt just behind me. I felt that I was pretty well trapped."

The girl gave a low moan, and Gordon, not daring to look up, hurried on with his story.

"There isn't much more to tell that you do not already know. I soon discovered the building was a church, not a prison. What happened afterward was the result of my extreme perturbance of mind, I suppose. I cannot account for my stupidity and subsequent cowardice in any other way. Neither was it possible for me to explain matters satisfactorily at any time during the whole mix-up, on account of the trust which I carried, and which I could on no account reveal even in confidence, or put in jeopardy in the slightest degree. Naturally at first my commission and how to get safely through it all was the only thing of importance to me. If you keep this in mind perhaps you will be able to judge me less harshly. My only thought when the carriage came to a halt was how to escape from those two pursuers, and that more or less pervaded my mind during what followed so that ordinary matters which at another time would have been at once clear to me, meant nothing at all. You see, the instant that carriage came to a standstill someone threw open the door, and I heard a voice call 'Where is the best man?' Then another voice said, 'Here he is!' I took it that they thought I was best man, but would soon discover that I wasn't when I came into the light. There wasn't any chance to slip away, or I should have done so, and vanished in the dark, but everybody surrounded me, and seemed to think I was all right. The two men who had followed were close behind eyeing me keenly. I'm satisfied that they were to blame for that wild ride we took in Pittsburgh! I soon saw by the remarks that the man I was supposed to be had been away from this country for ten years, and of course then they would not be very critical. I tried twice to explain that there was a mistake, but both times they misunderstood me and thought I was saying I couldn't go in the procession because

I hadn't practised. I don't just know how I came to be in such a dreadful mess. It would seem as if it ought to have been a very easy thing to say I had got into the wrong carriage and they must excuse me, that I wasn't their man, but, you see, they gave me no time to think nor to speak. They just turned me over from one man to another and took everything for granted, and I, finding that I would have to break loose and flee before their eyes if I wished to escape, reflected that there would be no harm in marching down the aisle as best man in a delayed wedding, if that was all there was to do. I could disappear as soon as the ceremony was over, and no one would be the wiser. The real best man would probably turn up and then they might wonder as they pleased for I would be far away and perhaps this was as good a place as any in which to hide for half an hour until my pursuers were baffled and well on their way seeking elsewhere for me. I can see now that I made a grave mistake in allowing even so much deception, but I did not see any harm in it then, and they all seemed in great distress for the ceremony to go forward. Bear in mind also that I was at that time entirely taken up with the importance of hiding my message until I could take it safely to my chief. Nothing else seemed to matter much. If the real best man was late to the wedding and they were willing to use me in his place what harm could come from it? He certainly deserved it for being late and if he came in during the ceremony he would think some one else had been put in his place. They introduced me to your brother — Jefferson. I thought he was the bridegroom, and I thought so until they laid your hand in mine!"

"Oh!" she moaned, and the little hand went to help its mate cover her face.

"I knew it!" he said bitterly. "I knew you would feel just that way as soon as you knew. I don't blame you. I deserve it! I was a fool, a villain, a dumb brute — whatever you have a mind to call me! You can't begin to understand how I have suffered for you since this happened, and how I have blamed myself."

He got up suddenly and strode over to the window, frowning down into the sunlit street, and wondering how it was that everybody seemed to be going on in exactly the same hurry as ever, when for him life had suddenly come to a standstill.

16

THE room was very still. The girl did not even sob. He
turned after a moment and went back to that bowed golden
head there in the deep crimson chair.

"Look here," he said, "I know you can't ever forgive me.
I don't expect it! I don't deserve it! But please don't feel so
awfully about it. I'll explain it all to every one. I'll make it
all right for you. I'll take every bit of blame on myself, and
get plenty of witnesses to prove all about it—"

The girl looked up with sorrow and surprise in her wet
eyes.

"Why, I do not blame you," she said, mournfully. "I cannot see how you were to blame. It was no one's fault. It was
just an unusual happening—a strange set of circumstances
I could not blame you. There is nothing to forgive, and if
there were I would gladly forgive it!"

"Then what on earth makes you look so white and feel so
distressed?" he asked in a distracted voice, as a man will sometimes look and talk to the woman he loves when she becomes
a tearful problem of despair to his obtuse eyes.

"Oh, don't you know?"

"No, I don't," he said. "You're surely not mourning for that brute of a man to whom you had promised to sacrifice your life?"

She shook her head, and buried her face in her hands again. He could see that the tears were dropping between her fingers, and they seemed to fall red hot upon his heart.

"Then what is it?" His tone was almost sharp in its demand, but she only cried the harder. Her slender shoulders were shaking with her grief now.

He put his hand down softly and touched her bowed head.

"Won't you tell me, Dear?" he breathed, and, stooping, knelt beside her.

The sobs ceased, and she was quite still for a moment, while his hand still lay on her hair with that gentle, pleading touch.

"It is—because you married me—in—that way—without knowing—Oh, can't you see how terrible—"

Oh, the folly and blindness of love! Gordon got up from his knees as if she had stung him.

"You need not feel bad about that any more," he said in a hurt tone. "Did I not tell you I would set you free at once? Surely no one in his senses could call you bound after such circumstances."

She was very still for an instant, as if he had struck her, and then she raised her golden head, and a pair of sweet eyes suddenly grown haughty.

"You mean that *I* will set *you* free!" she said coldly. "I could not think of letting you be bound by a misunderstanding when you were under great stress of mind. You were in no wise to blame. *I* will set *you* free."

"As you please," he retorted bitterly, turning toward the window again. "It all amounts to the same thing. There is nothing for you to feel bad about."

"Yes, there is," she answered, with a quick rush of feeling that broke through her assumed haughtiness. "I shall always feel that I have broken in upon your life. You have had a most trying experience with me, and you never can quite forget it. Things won't be the same—"

She paused and the quiet tears chased each other eloquently down her face.

"No," said Gordon still bitterly; "things will never be the same for me. I shall always see you sitting there in my chair. I shall always be missing you from it! But I am glad—glad. I would never have known what I missed if it had not been for this." He spoke almost savagely.

He did not look around, but she was staring at him in astonishment, her blue eyes suddenly alight.

"What do you mean?" she asked softly.

He wheeled around upon her. "I mean that I shall never forget you; that I do not want to forget you. I should rather have had these two days of your sweet company, than all my lifetime in any other companionship."

"Oh!" she breathed. "Then, why—why did you say what you did about being free?"

"I didn't say anything about being free that I remember. It was you that said that."

"I said I would set you free. I could not, of course, hold you to a bond you did not want—"

"But I did not say I did not want it. I said I would not hold you if *you* did not want to stay."

"Do you mean that if you had known me a little—that is, just as much as you know me now—and had come in there and found out your mistake before it was too late, that you would have *wanted* to go on with it?"

She waited for his answer breathlessly.

"If you had known me just as much as you do now, and had looked up and seen that it was I and not George Hayne you were marrying, would *you* have wanted to go on and be married?"

Her cheeks grew rosy and her eyes confused.

"I asked you first," she said, with just a flicker of a smile.

He caught the shimmer of light in her eyes, and came toward her eagerly, his own face all aglow now with a dawning understanding.

"Darling," he said, "I can go farther than you have asked. From the first minute my eyes rested upon your face under that mist of white veil I wished with all my heart that I might have known you before any other man had found and won you. When you turned and looked at me with that deep sorrow in your eyes, you pledged me with every fibre of my being to fight for you. I was yours from that instant. And when your little hand was laid in mine, my heart went out in longing to have it stay in mine forever. I know now, as I did not understand then, that the real reason for my not doing something to make known my identity at that instant was not because I was afraid of any of the things that might happen, or any scene I might make, but because my heart was fighting for the right to keep what had been given me out of the unknown. You are my wife, by every law of heaven and earth, if your heart will but say yes. I love you, as I never knew a man could love, and yet if you do not want to stay with me I will set you free; but it is true that I should never be the same, for I am married to you in my heart, and always shall be. Darling, look up and answer my question now."

He stood before her with outstretched arms, and for answer she rose and came to him slowly, with downcast eyes.

"I do not want to be set free," she said.

Then gently, tenderly, he folded his arms about her, as if she were too precious to handle roughly, and laid his lips upon hers.

It was the shrill, insistent clang of the telephone bell that broke in upon their bliss. For a moment Gordon let it ring, but its merciless clatter was not to be denied; so, drawing Celia close within his arm, he made her come with him to the 'phone.

To his annoyance, the haughty voice of Miss Bentley answered him from the little black distance of the 'phone.

His arm was about Celia, and she felt his whole body stiffen with formality.

"Oh, Miss Bentley! Good morning! Your message? Why no! Ah! Well, I have but just come in—"

A pause during which Celia, panic-stricken, handed him the paper on which she had written Julia's message.

"Ah! Oh, yes, I have the message. Yes, it is very kind of you—" he murmured stiffly, "but you will have to excuse me. No, really. It is utterly impossible! I have another engagement—" his arm stole closer around Celia's waist and caught her hand, holding it with a meaningful pressure. He smiled, with a grimace toward the telephone which gladdened her heart. "Pardon me, I didn't hear that," he went on. . . . "Oh, give up my engagement and come? . . . Not possibly!" His voice rang with a glad, decided force, and he held still closer the soft fingers in his hand. . . . "Well, I'm sorry you feel that way about it. I certainly am not trying to be disagreeable. No, I could not come to-morrow night either. . . . I cannot make any plan for the next few days. . . . I may have to leave town again. . . . It is quite possible I may have to return to New York. Yes, business has been very pressing. I hope you will excuse me. I am sorry to disappoint you. No, of course I didn't do it on purpose. I shall have some pleasant news to tell you when I see you again—or—" with a glance of deep love at Celia, "perhaps I shall find means to let you know of it before I see you."

The color came and went in Celia's cheeks. She understood what he meant and nestled closer to him.

"No, no, I could not tell it over the 'phone. No, it will keep. Good things will always keep if they are well cared for you know. No, really I can't. And I'm very sorry to disappoint you to-night, but it can't be helped. . . . Good-by."

He hung up the receiver with a sigh of relief.

"Who is Miss Bentley?" asked Celia, with natural interest. She was pleased that he had not addressed her as "Julia."

"Why, she is—a friend—I suppose you would call her. She

has been taking possession of my time lately rather more than I really enjoyed. Still, she is a nice girl. You'll like her, I think; but I hope you'll never get too intimate. I shouldn't like to have her continually around. She—" he paused and finished, laughing—"she makes me tired."

"I was afraid, from her tone when she 'phoned you, that she was a very dear friend—that she might be some one you cared for. There was a sort of proprietorship in her tone."

"Yes, that's the very word, proprietorship," he laughed. "I couldn't care for her. I never did. I tried to consider her in that light one day, because I'd been told repeatedly that I ought to settle down, but the thought of having her with me always was—well—intolerable. The fact is, you reign supreme in a heart that has never loved another girl. I didn't know there was such a thing as love like this. I knew I lacked something, but I didn't know what it was. This is greater than all the gifts of life, this gift of your love. And that it should come to me in this beautiful, unsought way seems too good to be true!"

He drew her to him once more and looked down into her lovely face, as if he could not drink enough of its sweetness.

"And to think you are willing to be my wife! My wife!" and he folded her close again.

A discreet tap on the door announced the arrival of the man Henry, and Gordon roused to the necessity of ordering lunch.

"Come in a minute, Henry," he said. "This is my wife. I hope you will henceforth take her wishes as your special charge, and do for her as you have done so faithfully for me."

The man's eyes shone with pleasure as he bowed low before the gentle lady.

"I is very glad to heah it, sah, and I offers you my congratchumlations, sah, and de lady, too. She can't find no bettah man in the whole United States dan Mars' Gordon. I's mighty glad you done got ma'ied, sah, an' I hopes you bof have a mighty fine life."

The luncheon was served in Henry's best style, and his dark face shone as he stepped noiselessly about, putting silver and china and glass in place, and casting admiring glances at the lady, who stood holding the little miniature in her hand and asking questions with a gentle voice:

"Your mother, you say? How dear she is! And she died so long ago! You never knew her? Oh, how strange and sweet and pitiful to have a beautiful girl-mother like that!"

She put out her hand to his in the shelter of the deep window, and they thought Henry did not see the look and touch that passed between them; but he discreetly averted his eyes and smiled benignly at the salt-cellars and the celery he was arranging. Then he hurried out to a florist's next door and returned with a dozen white roses, which he arranged in a queer little crystal pitcher, one of the few articles belonging to his mother that Gordon possessed. It had never been used before, except to stand on the mantel.

It was after they had finished their delightful luncheon, and Henry had cleared the table and left the room, that Gordon remarked:

"I wonder what has become of George Hayne? Do you suppose he means to try to make trouble?"

Celia's hands fluttered to her throat with a little gesture of fear.

"Oh!" she said. "I had forgotten him! How terrible! He will do *something*, of course. He will do *everything*. He will probably carry out all his threats. How could I have forgotten! Perhaps Mamma is now in great distress. What can we do? What can *I* do?"

"Don't be frightened," he soothed her. "He cannot do anything very dreadful, and if he tries we'll soon silence him. What he has written in those letters is blackmail. He is simply a big coward, who will run and hide as soon as he is exposed. He thought you did not understand law, and so took advantage of you. I'm sure I can silence him."

"Oh, do you think so? But Mamma! Poor Mamma! It will

kill her! And George will stop at nothing when he is crossed. I have known him too long. It will be *terrible* if he carries out his threat." Tears were in her eyes, agony was in her face.

"We must telephone your mother at once and set her heart at rest. Then we can find out just what ought to be done," said Gordon soothingly. "It was unforgivably thoughtless in me not to have done it before."

Celia's face was radiant at the thought of speaking to her mother.

"Oh, how beautiful! Why didn't I think of that before? What perfectly dear things telephones are!"

With one accord, they went to the telephone table.

"Shall you call them up, or shall I?" he asked.

"You call, and then I will speak to Mamma," she said, her eyes shining with her joy in him. "I want them to hear your voice again. They can't help knowing you are all right when they hear your voice."

For that, he gave her a glance very much worth having.

"Just how do you account for the fact that you didn't think I was all right yesterday afternoon? I have a very realizing sense that you didn't. I used my voice to the best of my ability, but it did no good then."

"Well, you see, that was different! There were those letters to be accounted for. Mamma and Jeff don't know anything about the letters."

"And what are you going to tell them now?"

She drew her brows down a minute and thought.

"You'd better find out how much they already know," he suggested. "If this George Hayne hasn't turned up yet, perhaps you can wait until you can write, or we might be able to go up to-morrow and explain it ourselves."

"Oh, could we? How lovely!"

"I think we could," said Gordon. "I'm sure I can make it possible. Of course, you know a wedding journey isn't exactly in the program of the Secret Service, but I might be able to work them for one. I surely can in a few days if this Holman business doesn't hold me up. I may be needed for a witness. I'll have to talk with the chief first."

"Oh, how perfectly beautiful! Then you call them up, and just say something pleasant — anything, you know, and then say I'll speak to Mamma."

She gave him the number, and in a few minutes a voice from New York said, "Hello!"

"Hello!" called Gordon. "Is this Mr. Jefferson Hathaway? . . . Well, this is your new brother-in-law. How are you all? . . . Your mother recovered from all the excitement and weariness? . . . That's good. . . . What's that? . . . You've been trying to 'phone us in Chicago? . . . But we're not in Chicago. We changed our minds and came to Washington instead. . . . Yes, we're in Washington—The Harris Apartments. We have been very selfish not to have communicated with you sooner. At least I have. Celia hasn't had any choice in the matter. I've kept her so busy. Yes, she's very well, and seems to look happy. She wants to speak for herself. I'll try to arrange to bring her up to-morrow for a little visit. I want to see you too. We've a lot of things to explain to you. . . . Here is Celia. She wants to speak to you."

Celia, her eyes shining, her lips quivering with suppressed excitement, took the receiver.

"Oh, Jeff dear, it's good to hear your voice," she said. "Is everything all right? Yes, I've been having a perfectly beautiful time, and I've something fine to tell you. All those nice things you said to me just before you got off the train are true. Yes, he's just as nice as you said, and a great deal nicer besides. Oh, yes, I'm very happy, and I want to speak to Mamma please. Jeff, is she all right? Is she *perfectly* well, and not fretting a bit? You know you promised to tell me. What's that? She thought I looked sad? Well, I did but that's all gone now. Everything is perfectly beautiful. Tell mother to come to the 'phone please — I want to make her understand."

"I'm going to tell her, dear," she whispered, looking up at

Gordon. "I'm afraid George will get there before we do and make her worry."

For answer he stooped and kissed her, his arm encircling her and drawing her close. "Whatever you think best, dearest," he whispered back.

"Is that you, Mamma?" With a happy smile she turned back to the 'phone. "Dear Mamma! Yes, I'm all safe and happy, and I'm sorry you have worried. We won't let you do it again. But listen; I've something to tell you, a surprise—Mamma, I did not marry George Hayne at all. No, I say I *did not* marry George Hayne at all. George Hayne is a wicked man. I can't tell you about it over the 'phone but that was why I looked sad. Yes, I was *married* all right, but not to George. He's oh, so different, Mother you can't think. He's right here beside me now, and Mother, he is just as dear—you'd be very happy about him if you could see him. What did you say? Didn't I mean to marry George? Why Mother, I never wanted to. I was awfully unhappy about it, and I knew I made you feel so too, though I tried not to. But I'll explain all about it. . . . No, there's nothing whatever for you to worry about. Everything is right now and life looks more beautiful to me than it ever did before. What's his name? Oh;" she looked up at Gordon with a funny little expression of dismay. She had forgotten and he whispered it in her ear.

"Cyril—"

"It's Cyril, Mother! Isn't that a pretty name! Which name? Oh, the first name of course. That last name?"

"Gordon—" he supplied in her ear again.

"Cyril Gordon, Mother," she said, giggling in spite of herself at her strange predicament. . . . "Yes, Mother. I am very, very happy. I couldn't be happier unless I had you and Jeff, too, and"—she paused, hesitating at the unaccustomed name,—"and Cyril says we're coming to visit you tomorrow. We'll come up and see you and explain everything. And you're not to worry about George Hayne if he comes.

Just let Jeff put him off by telling him you have sent for me, or something of the sort, and don't pay any attention to what he says. What? You say he did come? How strange — and he hasn't been back? I'm so thankful. He is dreadful. Oh, Mother, you don't know what I've escaped! And Cyril is good and dear. What? You want to speak to him? All right. He's right here. Good-by, Mother, dear, till to-morrow. And you'll promise not to worry about anything? All right. Here is — Cyril."

Gordon took the receiver.

"Mother, I'm taking good care of her, just as I promised, and I'm going to bring her for a flying visit up to see you to-morrow. Yes, I'll take good care of her. She is very dear to me. The best thing that ever came into my life."

Then a mother's blessing came thrilling over the wires, and touched the handsome, manly face with tenderness.

"Thank you," he said. "I shall try always to make you glad you said those words."

They returned to looking in each other's eyes, after the receiver was hung up, as if they had been parted a long time. It seemed somehow as if their joy must be greater than any other married couple, because they had all their courting yet to do. It was beautiful to think of what was before them.

There was so much on both sides to be told; and to be told over again because only half had been told; and there were so many hopes and experiences to be exchanged; so many opinions to compare, and to rejoice over because they were alike on many essentials. Then there were the rooms to be gone through, and Gordon's pictures and favorite books to look at and talk about, and plans for the future to be touched upon — just barely touched upon.

The apartment would do until they could look about and get a house, Gordon said, his heart swelling with the proud thought that at last he would have a real home, like his other married friends, with a real princess to preside over it.

Then Celia had to tell all about the horror of the last three

months, with the unpleasant shadows of the preceding years
back of it. She told this in the dusk of the evening, before
Henry had come in to light up, and before they had realized
that it was almost dinner-time. She told it with her face hidden on her husband's shoulder, and his arms close about her,
to give her comfort at each revelation of the story. They tried
also to plan what to do about George Hayne; and then there
was the whole story of Gordon's journey and commission
from the time the old chief had called him into the office until
he came to stand beside her at the church altar and they were
married. It was told in careful detail with all the comical, exasperating and pitiful incidents of white dog and little newsboy; but the strangest part about it all was that Gordon never
said one word about Julia Bentley and her imaginary presence with him that first day, and he never even knew that he
had left out an important detail.

Celia laughed over the white dog and declared they must
bring him home to live with them; and she cried over the
story of the brave little newsboy and was eager to visit him
in New York, promising herself all sorts of pleasure in taking him gifts and permanently bettering his condition; and
it was in this way that Gordon incidentally learned that his
wife had a fortune in her own right, a fact that for a time gave
him great uneasiness of mind until she had soothed him and
laughed at him for an hour or more; for Gordon was an independent creature and had ideas about supporting his wife
by his own toil. Besides, it seemed an unfair advantage to
have taken a wife and a fortune as it were unaware.

But Celia's fortune had not spoiled her, and she soon made
him see that it had always been a mere incident in her scheme
of living; a comfortable and pleasant incident to be sure, but
still an incident to be kept always in the background, and
never for a moment to be a cause for self-congratulation or
pride.

Gordon found himself dreading the explanation that
would have to come when he reached New York and faced

his wife's mother and brother. Celia had accepted his explanations, because, somehow by the beautiful ways of the spirit, her soul had found and believed in his soul before the truth was made known to her, but would her mother and brother be able also to believe? And he fell to planning with Celia just how he should tell the story; and this led to his bringing out a number of letters and papers that would be worth while showing as credentials, and every step of the way, as Celia got glimpse after glimpse into his past, her face shone with joy and her heart leaped with the assurance that her lot had been cast in goodly places, for she perceived not only that this man was honored and respected in high places, but that his early life had been peculiarly pure and true.

The strange loneliness that had surrounded his young manhood seemed suddenly to have broken ahead of him, and to have opened out into the glory of the companionship of one peculiarly fitted to fill the need of his life. Thus they looked into one another's eyes reading their life-joy, and entered into the beautiful miracle of acquaintanceship.

17

THE next morning quite early the 'phone called Gordon to the office. The chief's secretary said the matter was urgent.

He hurried away leaving Celia somewhat anxious lest their plans for going to New York that day could not be carried out, but she made up her mind not to fret even if the trip had to be put off a little, and solaced herself with a short visit with her mother over the telephone.

Gordon entered his chief's office a trifle anxiously, for he felt that in justice to his wife he ought to take her right back to New York and get matters there adjusted; but he feared that there would be business to hold him at home until the Holman matter was settled.

The chief greeted him affably and bade him sit down.

"I am sorry to have called you up so early," he said, "but we need you. The fact is, they've arrested Holman and five other men, and you are in immediate demand to identify them. Would it be asking too much of an already over-worked man to send you back to New York to-day?"

Gordon almost sprang from his seat in pleasure.

"It just exactly fits in with my plans, or, rather, my wishes," he said, smiling. "There are several matters of my own that

I would like to attend to in New York and for which of course I did not have time."

He paused and looked at his chief, half hesitating, marvelling that the way had so miraculously opened for him to keep silence a little longer on the subject of his marriage. Perhaps the chief need never be told that the marriage ceremony took place on the day of the Holman dinner.

"That is good," said the chief, smiling. "You certainly have earned the right to attend to your own affairs. Then we need not feel so bad at having to send you back. Can you go on the afternoon train? Good! Then let us hear your account of your trip briefly, to see if there are any points we didn't notice yesterday. But first just step here a moment. I have something to show you."

He flung open the door to the next office.

"You knew that Ferry had left the Department on account of his ill-health? I have taken the liberty of having your things moved in here. This will hereafter be your headquarters, and you will be next to me in the Department."

Gordon turned in amazement and gazed at the kindly old face. Promotion he had hoped for, but such promotion, right over the heads of his elders and superiors, he had never dreamed of receiving. He could have taken the chief in his arms.

"Pooh! Pooh!" said the chief. "You deserve it, you deserve it!" when Godon tried to blunder out some words of appreciation. Then, as if to cap the climax, he added:

"And, by the way, you know some one has got to run across the water to look after that Stanhope matter. That will fall to you, I'm afraid. Sorry to keep you trotting around the globe, but perhaps you'll like to make a little vacation of it. The Department'll give you some time if you want it. Oh, don't thank me! It's simply the reward of doing your duty, to have more duties given you, and higher ones. You have done well, young man. I have here all the papers in the Stanhope case, and full directions written out, and then if you can plan for it you needn't return, unless it suits your pleasure. You understand the matter as fully as I do already. And now for business. Let's hurry through. There are one or two little matters we must talk over and I know you will want to hurry back and get ready for your journey." And so after all the account of Gordon's extraordinary escape and eventful journey home became by reason of its hasty repetition a most prosaic story composed of the bare facts and not all of those.

At parting the chief pressed Gordon's hand with heartiness and ushered him out into the hall, with the same brusque manner he used to close all business interviews, and Gordon found himself hurrying through the familiar halls in a daze of happiness, the secret of his unexpected marriage still his own — and hers.

Celia was watching at the window when his key clicked in the lock and he let himself into the apartment his face alight with the joy of meeting her again after the brief absence. She turned in a quiver of pleasure at his coming.

"Well, get ready," he said joyfully. "We are ordered off to New York on the afternoon train, with a wedding trip to Europe into the bargain; and I'm promoted to the next place to the chief. What do you think of that for a morning's surprise?"

He tossed up his hat like a boy, came over to where she stood, and stooping laid reverent lips upon her brow and eyes.

"Oh, beautiful! Lovely!" cried Celia, ecstatically. "Come sit down on the couch and tell me all about it. We can work faster afterward if we get it off our minds. Was your chief much shocked that you were married without his permission or knowledge?"

"Why, that was the best of all. I didn't have to tell him I was married. And he is not to know until just as I sail. He need never know how it all happened. It isn't his business and it would be hard to explain. No one need ever know except your mother and brother unless you wish them to, dear."

"Oh, I am so glad and relieved," said Celia, delightedly. "I've been worrying about that a little, — what people would think of us, — for of course we couldn't possibly explain it all out as it is to us. They would always be watching us to see if we really cared for each other; and suspecting that we didn't, and it would be horrid. I think it is our own precious secret, and nobody but Mamma and Jeff have a right to know, don't you?"

"I certainly do, and I was casting about in my mind as I went into the office how I could manage not to tell the chief, when what did he do but spring a proposition on me to go at once to New York and identify those men. He apologized tremendously for having to send me right back again, but said it was necessary. I told him it just suited me for I had affairs of my own that I had not had time to attend to when I was there, and would be glad to go back and see to them. That let me out on the wedding question for it would be only necessary to tell him I was married when I got back. He would never ask when."

"But the announcements," said Celia catching her breath laughingly, "I never thought of that. We'll just have to have some kind of announcements or my friends will not understand about my new name; and we'll have to send him one, won't we?"

"Why, I don't know. Couldn't we get along without announcements? You can explain to your intimate friends, and the others won't ever remember the name after a few months — we'll not be likely to meet many of them right away. I'll write to my chief and tell him informally leaving out the date entirely. He won't miss it. If we have announcements at all we needn't send him one. He wouldn't be likely ever to see one any other way, or to notice the date. I think we can manage that matter. We'll talk it over with your—' he hesitated and then smiling tenderly added, "we'll talk it over with *Mother*. How good it sounds to say that. I never knew my mother, you know."

Celia nestled her hands in his and murmured, "Oh, I am so happy, — so happy! But I don't understand how you got a wedding trip without telling your chief about our marriage."

"Easy as anything. He asked me if I would mind running across the water to attend to a matter for the Service and said I might have extra time while there for a vacation. He never suspects that vacation is to be used as a wedding trip. I'll write him, or 'phone him the night we leave New York. I may have to stay in the city two or three days to get this Holman matter settled, and then we can be off. In the meantime you can spend the time reconciling your mother to her new son. Do you think we'll have a very hard time explaining matters to her?"

"Not a bit," said Celia, gaily. "She never did like George. It was the only thing we ever disagreed about, my marrying him. She suspected all the time I wasn't happy and couldn't understand why I insisted on marrying him when I hadn't seen him for ten years. She begged me to wait until he had been back in the country for a year or two, but he would not hear to such a thing and threatened to carry out his worst at once."

Gordon's heart suddenly contracted with righteous wrath over the cowardliness of the man who sought to gain his own ends by intimidating a woman — and this woman, so dear, so beautiful, so lovely in her nature. It seemed the man's heart must indeed be black to have done what he did. He mentally resolved to search him out and bring him to justice as soon as he reached New York. It puzzled him to understand how easily he seemed to have abandoned his purposes. Perhaps after all he was more of a coward than they thought, and had not dared to remain in the country when he found that Celia had braved his wrath and married another man. He would find out about him and set the girl's heart at rest just as soon as possible, that any embarrassment at some future time might be avoided. Gordon stooped and kissed his wife again, a caress that seemed to promise all reparation for the past.

But it suddenly occurred to the two that trains did not wait for lovers' long loitering, and with one accord they went to work. Celia of course had very little preparation to make. Her trunk was probably in Chicago and would need to be wired for. Gordon attended to that the first thing, looking up the number of the check and ordering it back to New York by telegraph. Turning from the telephone he rang for the man and asked Celia to give the order for lunch while he got together some things that he must take with him. A stay of several weeks would necessitate a little more baggage than he had taken to New York.

He went into the bedroom and began pulling out things to pack but when Celia turned from giving her directions she found him standing in the bedroom doorway with an old-fashioned velvet jewel case in his hand which he had just taken from the little safe in his room. His face wore a wonderful tender light as if he had just discovered something precious.

"Dear," he said. "I wonder if you will care for these. They were mother's. Perhaps this ring will do until I can buy you a new one. See if it will fit you. It was my mother's."

He held out a ring containing a diamond of singular purity and brilliance in quaint old-fashioned setting.

Celia put out her hand with its wedding ring, the ring that he had put upon her finger at the altar, and he slipped the other jewelled one above it. It fitted perfectly.

"It is a beauty," breathed Celia, holding out her hand to admire it, "and I would far rather have it than a new one. Your dear little mother!"

"There's not much else here but a little string of pearls and a pin or two. I have always kept them near me. Somehow they seemed like a link between me and mother. I was keeping them for—" he hesitated and then giving her a rare smile he finished:

"I was keeping them for you."

Her answering look was eloquent, and needed no words, which was well, for Henry appeared at that moment to serve luncheon and remind his master that his train left in a little over two hours. There was no further time for sentiment.

And yet, these two, it seemed, could not be practical that day. They idled over their luncheon and dawdled over their packing, stopping to look at this and that picture or bit of bric-a-brac that Gordon had picked up in some of his travels; and Henry finally had to take things in his own hands, pack them off and send their baggage after them. Henry was a capable man and rejoiced to see the devotion of his master and his new mistress, but he had a practical head and knew where his part came in.

18

THE journey back to New York seemed all too brief for the two whose lives had just been blended so unexpectedly, and every mile was filled with a new and sweet discovery of delight in one another; and then, when they reached the city they rushed in on Mrs. Hathaway and the eager young Jeff like two children who had so much to tell they did not know where to begin.

Mrs. Hathaway settled the matter by insisting on their going to dinner immediately and leaving all explanations until afterward; and with the servants present of course there was little that could be said about the matter that each one had most at heart. But there was a spirit of deep happiness in the atmosphere and one couldn't possibly entertain any fears under the influence of the radiant smiles that passed between mother and daughter, husband and wife, brother and sister.

As soon as the meal was concluded the mother led them up to her private sitting room, and closing the door she stood facing them all as half breathless with the excitement of the moment they stood in a row before her:

"My three dear children!" she murmured. Gordon's eye

lit with joy and his heart thrilled with the wonder of it all. Then the mother stepped up to him and placing her hand on his arm led him over to the couch and made him sit beside her, while the brother and sister sat down together close by.

"Now, Cyril, my new son," said she, deliberately, her eyes resting approvingly upon his face, "you may tell me your story. I see my girl has lost both head and heart to you and I doubt if she could tell it connectedly."

And while Celia and Jeff were laughing at this, Gordon set about his task of winning a mother, and incidentally an eager-eyed young brother who was more than half committed to his cause already.

Celia watched proudly as her handsome husband took out his credentials, and began his explanation.

"First, I must tell you who I am, and these papers will do it better than I could. Will you look at them, please?"

He handed her a few letters and papers.

"These papers on the top show the rank and position that my father and my grandfather held with the government and in the army. This is a letter from the president to my father congratulating him on his approaching marriage with my mother. That paper contains my mother's family tree, and the letters with it will give an idea of the honor in which my mother's family was held in Washington and in Virginia, her old home. I know these matters are not of much moment, and say nothing whatever about what I am myself, but they are things you would have been likely to know about my family if you had known me all my life; and at least they will tell you that my family was respectable."

Mrs. Hathaway was examining the papers, and suddenly looked up exclaiming: "My dear! My father knew your grandfather. I think I saw him once when he came to our home in New York. It was years ago and I was a young girl, but I remember he was a fine looking man with keen dark eyes and a heavy head of iron gray hair."

She looked at Gordon keenly.

"I wonder if your eyes are not like his. It was long ago of course."

"They used to say I looked like him. I do not remember him. He died when I was very young."

The mother looked up with a pleased smile.

"Now tell me about yourself," she said and laid a gentle hand on his.

Gordon looked down, an embarrassed flush spreading over his face.

"There's nothing great to tell," he said. "I've always tried to live a straight true life, and I've never been in love with any girl before—" he flashed a wonderful, blinding smile upon Celia.

"I was left alone in the world when quite young and have lived around in boarding-schools and college. I'm a graduate of Harvard and I've travelled a little. There was some money left from my father's estate, not much. I'm not rich. I'm a Secret Service man, and I love my work. I get a good salary and was this morning promoted to the position next in rank to my chief, so that now I shall have still more money. I shall be able to make your daughter comfortable and give her some of the luxuries, if not all, to which she has been accustomed."

"My dear boy, that part is not what I am anxious about—" interrupted the mother.

"I know," said Gordon, "But it is a detail you have a right to be told. I understand that you care far more what I am than how much money I can make, and I promise you I am going to try to be all that you would want your daughter's husband to be. Perhaps the best thing I can say for myself is that I love her better than my life, and I mean to make her happiness the dearest thing in life to me."

The mother's look of deep understanding answered him more eloquently than words could have done, and after a moment she spoke again.

"But I do not understand how you could have known one another and I never have heard of you. Celia is not good at keeping things from her mother, though the last three months she has had a sadness that I could not fathom, and was forced to lay to her natural dread of leaving home. She seemed so insistent upon having this marriage just as George planned it—and I was so afraid she would regret not waiting. How could you have known one another all this time and she never talked to me about it, and why did George Hayne have any part whatever in it if you two loved one another? Just how long have you known each other any way? Did it begin when you visited in Washington last spring, Celia?"

With dancing eyes Celia shook her head.

"No, Mamma. If I had met him then I'm sure George Hayne would never had had anything to do with the matter, for Cyril would have known how to help me out of my difficulty."

"I shall have to tell you the whole story from my standpoint, and from the beginning," said Gordon, dreading now that the crisis was upon him, what the outcome would be. "I have wanted you to know who and what I was before you know the story, that you might judge me as kindly as possible, and know that however I may have been to blame in the matter it was through no intention of mine. My story may sound rather impossible. I know it will seem improbable, but it is nevertheless true, everything that I have to tell. May I hope to be believed?"

"I think you may," answered the mother searching his face anxiously. "Those eyes of yours are not lying eyes."

"Thank you," he said simply, and then gathering all his courage he plunged into his story.

Mrs. Hathaway was watching him with searching interest. Jeff had drawn his chair up close and could scarcely restrain his excitement, and when Gordon told of his commission he burst forth explosively:

"Gee! But that was a great stunt! I'd have liked to have been along with you! You must be simply great to be trusted with a thing like that!"

But his mother gently reproved him:

"Hush, my son, let us hear the story."

Celia sat quietly watching her husband with pride, two bright spots of color of her cheeks, and her hands clasping each other tightly. She was hearing many details now that were new to her. Once more, when Gordon mentioned the dinner at Holman's Jeff interrupted with:

"Holman! Holman! Not J. P.? Why of course—we know him! Celia was one of his daughter's bridesmaids last spring. The old lynx! I always thought he was crooked! People hint a lot of things about him—"

"Jeff, dear, let us hear the story," again insisted his mother and the story continued.

Gordon had been looking down as he talked. He dreaded to see their faces as the truth should dawn upon them, but when he had told all he lifted honest eyes to the white-faced mother and pleaded with her:

"Indeed, indeed, I hope you will believe me, that not until they laid your daughter's hand in mine did I know that I was supposed to be the bridegroom. I thought all the time her brother was the bridegroom. If I had not been so distraught, and trying so hard to think how to escape, I suppose I would have noticed that I was standing next to her and that everything was peculiar about the whole matter, but I didn't. And then when I suddenly knew that she and I were being married, what should I have done? Do you think I ought to have stopped the ceremony then and there and made a scene before all those people? What was the right thing to do? Suppose my commission had been entirely out of the question, and I had had no duty toward the government to keep entirely quiet about myself, do you think I ought to have made a scene? Would you have wanted me to for your daughter's sake? Tell me please," he insisted, gently.

And while she hesitated he added:

"I did some pretty hard thinking during that first quarter of a second that I realized what was happening, and I tell you honestly I didn't know what was the right thing to do. It seemed awful for her sake to make a scene, and to tell you the truth I worshipped her from the moment my eyes rested upon her. There was something sad and appealing as she looked at me that seemed to pledge my very life to save her from trouble. Tell me, do you think I ought to have stopped the ceremony then at the first moment of my realization that I was being married?"

The mother's face had softened as she watched him and listened to his tender words about Celia and now she answered gently:

"I am not sure — perhaps not! It was a very grave question to face. I don't know that I can blame you for doing nothing. It would have been terrible for her and us and everybody and have made it all so public. Oh, I think you did right not to do anything publicly — perhaps — and yet — it is terrible to me to think you have been forced to marry my daughter in that way."

"Please do not say forced, —" said Gordon laying both hands earnestly upon hers and looking into her eyes, "I tell you one thing that held me back from doing anything was that I so earnestly desired that what I was passing through might be real and lasting. I have never seen one like her before. I know that if the mistake had been righted and she had passed out of my life I should never have felt the same again. I am glad, glad with all my heart that she is mine, and — Mother! — I think she is glad too!"

The mother turned toward her daughter, and Celia with starry eyes came and knelt before them, and laid her hands in the hands of her husband, saying with ringing voice:

"Yes, dear little Mother, I am gladder than I ever was before in my life."

And kneeling thus, with her husband's arm about her, her

face against his shoulder, and both her hands clasped in his, she told her mother about the tortures that George Hayne had put her through, until the mother turned white with horror at what her beloved and cherished child had been enduring, and the brother got up and stormed across the floor, vowing vengeance on the luckless head of poor George Hayne.

Then after the mother had given her blessing to the two and Jeff had added an original one of his own, there was the whole story of the eventful wedding trip to tell, which they both told by solos and choruses until the hour grew alarmingly late and the mother suddenly sent them all off to bed.

The next few days were both busy and happy ones for the two. They went to the hospital and gladdened the life of the little newsboy with fruit and toys and many promises; and they brought home a happy white dog from his boarding place whom Jeff adopted as his own. Gordon had a trying hour or two at court with his one-time host, the scoundrel who had stolen the cipher message; and the thick-set man glared at him from a cell window as he passed along the corridor of the prison whither he had gone in search of George Hayne.

Gordon, in his search for the lost bridegroom, whom for many reasons he desired to find as soon as possible, had asked the help of one of the men at work on the Holman case, in searching for a certain George Hayne who needed very much to be brought to justice.

"Oh, you won't have to search for him," declared the man with a smile. "He's safely landed in prison three days ago. He was caught as neatly as rolling off a log by the son of the man whose name he forged several years ago. It was trust money of a big corporation and the man died in his place in a prison cell, but the son means to see the real culprit punished."

And so Gordon, in the capacity of Celia's lawyer, went to the prison to talk with George Hayne, and that miserable man found no excuse for his sins when the searching talk was over. Gordon did not let the man know who he was, and merely made it understood that Celia was married, and that if he attempted to make her any further trouble the whole thing would be exposed and he would have to answer a grave charge of blackmail.

The days passed rapidly, and at last the New York matter for which Gordon's presence was needed was finished, and he was free to sail away with his bride. On the morning of their departure Gordon's voice rang out over the miles of telephone wires to his old chief in Washington: "I am married and am just starting on my wedding trip. Don't you want to congratulate me?" And the old chief's gruff voice sounded back:

"Good work, old man! Congratulations for you both. She may or may not be the best girl in all the world; I haven't had a chance to see yet; but she's a lucky girl, for she's got *the best man I know.* Tell her that for me! Bless you both! I'm glad she's going with you. It won't be so lonesome."

Gordon gave her the message that afternoon as they sailed straight into the sunshine of a new and beautiful life together.

"Dear," he said, as he arranged her steamer rug more comfortably about her, "has it occurred to you that you are probably the only bride who ever married the best man at her wedding?"

Celia smiled appreciatively and after a minute replied mischievously:

"I suppose every bride *thinks* her husband is the best man."

About the Author

Grace Livingston Hill is well known as one of the most prolific writers of romantic fiction. Her personal life was fraught with joys and sorrows not unlike those experienced by many of her fictional heroines.

Born in Wellsville, New York, Grace nearly died during the first hours of life. But her loving parents and friends turned to God in prayer. She survived miraculously, thus her thankful father named her Grace.

Grace was always close to her father, a Presbyterian minister, and her mother, a published writer. It was from them that she learned the art of storytelling. When Grace was twelve, a close aunt surprised her with a hardbound, illustrated copy of one of Grace's stories. This was the beginning of Grace's journey into being a published author.

In 1892 Grace married Fred Hill, a young minister, and they soon had two lovely young daughters. Then came 1901, a difficult year for Grace — the year when, within months of each other, both her father and husband died. Suddenly Grace had to find a new place to live (her home was owned by the church where her husband had been pastor). It was a struggle for Grace to raise her young daughters alone, but through everything she kept writing. In 1902 she produced *The Angel of His Presence, The Story of a Whim,* and *An Unwilling Guest.* In 1903 her two books *According to the Pattern* and *Because of Stephen* were published.

It wasn't long before Grace was a well-known author, but she wanted to go beyond just entertaining her readers. She soon included the message of God's salvation through Jesus Christ in each of her books. For Grace, the most important thing she did was not write books but share the message of salvation, a message she felt God wanted her to share through the abilities he had given her.

In all, Grace Livingston Hill wrote more than one hundred books, all of which have sold thousands of copies and have touched the lives of readers around the world with their message of "enduring love" and the true way to lasting happiness: a relationship with God through his Son, Jesus Christ.

In an interview shortly before her death, Grace's devotion to her Lord still shone clear. She commented that whatever she had accomplished had been God's doing. She was only his servant, one who had tried to follow his teaching in all her thoughts and writing.